JEREMY
VISICK

JEREMY VISICK

◆ ◆ ◆

David Wiseman

HOUGHTON MIFFLIN COMPANY
BOSTON

J
W

Library of Congress Cataloging-in-Publication Data

Wiseman, David.
  Jeremy Visick.
  Summary: Twelve-year-old Matthew is drawn almost against his will to help a boy his own age who was lost in a mining disaster a century before.
  ISBN 0-395-30449-0
  [1. Space and time—Fiction. 2. Miners—Fiction. 3. Cornwall, Eng.—Fiction]
I. Title.
PZ7.W78024Je   80-28116
[Fic]

Printed in the United States of America

RNF ISBN 0-395-30449-0
PAP ISBN 0-395-56153-1

AGM 10 9 8 7 6 5 4 3 2 1

FOR

PICCOLO, SALLY, PATRICK, AND DEBORAH,
who enjoyed other stories I told them
and who will want to share in this

·I·

"IT'S RUBBISH, SIR."

"What is, young Clemens?" George Williams looked with mild irritation at this member of his new class.

"History, sir. Dates and things like that." Matthew Clemens looked at his teacher and shook his head in gentle rebuke at the dark look of annoyance that was beginning to spread over Mr. Williams's face.

"Well now. So that's what you think. Who agrees with him, eh?" George Williams asked, and was not surprised to find Matthew Clemens enjoying general support. He allowed a moment of noisy acclaim for Clemens's viewpoint.

"So," he interrupted. "Dates and things like that — your idea of history — is rubbish. We shall see." He stopped and looked out of the window of his classroom. His room at the corner of the building, a new comprehensive school, overlooked green fields and, beyond, the sprawling estates of the town.

"Stand up, Clemens," Williams said quietly.

Clemens stood, a sturdy figure, brown curly hair

untidily falling over a round, cheerful face. "Yes, sir," he said with mock humility.

"Come here," the teacher said.

Matthew Clemens warily approached. He was not sure of Mr. Williams. This was the first time the class had met him.

"Stand by me. Come on, boy. I won't bite."

Matthew drew near with exaggerated caution. The class giggled, but quieted down when Mr. Williams looked hard at them.

"Look out of the window, Clemens." Williams went back to his desk and sat there. "Tell us what you see."

There was silence from Matthew, a bewildered silence. "What I see, sir?"

"What you see, Clemens. Describe to us all the things you can see."

Matthew responded brightly. "Mr. Stevens on the rugby field with the fourth-year class. Pengilly's playing up, sir. Mr. Stevens is ticking him off."

The class giggled again.

"Beyond the field, Clemens. Look further than the end of your nose, Clemens. What's out there?"

"Houses, sir — streets, people, chimneys."

"Chimneys, eh? What sort of chimneys?"

"All sorts, sir. A big one there, a tall chimney, and fat."

"Describe it, Clemens."

"It's built of stone, in three stages, sort of."

"What is it, Clemens? Any idea?"

"The stack of an old engine house?"

"Yes?"

Matthew shook his head. He had told him all he knew. What else was there to know? He looked at Mr. Williams and began to move away from the window, back to his seat.

"No," said Williams. "We're not finished. Does anyone know about the chimney stack?"

A hand was raised.

"Mary?"

"Pednandrea, sir. That was the name of the mine — an old tin mine."

"Good. What else can you see, Clemens?"

"The railway, a viaduct. There's a train going over it."

"What else?"

"Houses. A chapel or something like that."

"It's all history out there, Clemens. Your history, my history. You and me, boy, not dates and things. You and me. That's what history is all about. How we came to be here, in the way we are, the clothes we wear." He looked down at himself and wished he hadn't spoken. He was notorious, he knew, as the untidiest member of the staff. The class laughed at the rueful look on his face as he glanced at his baggy, old-style flannels and his out-of-date, shabby sports coat.

He laughed with them.

"Yes," he said, anticipating Clemens's comment, as

he saw from the mischievous glint in the boy's eyes. "You're right, Clemens. My clothes are a part of history. They'd be better in a museum, I expect. But that's what history deals with, as well as dates and things. Real things. The work you do, the food you eat, the homes you build, the way you live, the way you die."

He had caught their interest. Clemens had quietly returned to his seat and was listening intently.

"The way you die," repeated Williams and paused a moment. "You live at Gwennap, don't you, Clemens?"

Matthew nodded.

"Have you ever looked around the churchyard there?"

Matthew shook his head. He had no desire to go into the churchyard. It seemed to him a gloomy, forbidding place. He had walked through it once, under the avenue of yew trees; the trees had dripped with mist and the grassy mounds underfoot had been clinging wet. The tombstones stood awry and displaced, with gaps yawning between the slabs of some of the larger monuments and dark, ivy-fringed holes leading to the mysteries of the vaults below. He shuddered at the recollection of it. He shook his head again, emphatically.

"Not likely, sir," he said.

"I want you to go there this weekend, then. Make it your special homework for me and report back to us next week. Go to the western end of the church and outside look among the tombstones until you find one to a family called Martin. Copy what you see there and report back on Tuesday, our next lesson."

"Please, sir." Matthew sounded uncertain.

Williams looked closely at him. "Well, Clemens?"

Matthew hesitated. He could not admit he was scared.

"Nothing, sir," he said.

"Right," said Williams. "Let's go on."

◆ ◆ ◆

Matthew Clemens left the school bus at the corner of the main road. He walked for a little way up the lane with Mary Thomas, who lived at the farm nearby.

"How did you know about that chimney stack?" he asked.

"Pednandrea?" she said.

"Whatever it's called." He pretended to be indifferent, but he was interested and could not hide his curiosity.

"My dad told me about it. He knows a lot about the mines. He's got lots of books to do with them, and rock specimens, and old mining tools and things."

They stood at the granite-pillared entrance to the farmyard. The farm buildings were old and solid-walled, as was the farmhouse, simple and modest though it was.

"Are you interested?" said Mary.

"Maybe."

5

"Dad'll talk the hind leg off a donkey if you give him half a chance. Come and see him."

"Not now," said Matthew. "Some other time." He turned and ran along the lane, under the trees and beside the stream, until he came to his family's cottage.

It was set back from the road. To reach it he had to cross the stream. At one time — not long back, said his mother, but before they had come to live here — the house had drawn its water from the stream, for drinking as well as for washing. Now they were on the mains supply and only used the water in the stream for washing their old car.

Their cottage had once been two homes for two families, but some years ago the two had been torn out inside and now it was a single house, home for his parents, his older sister, Janet, and himself. It was a squat building, warm and cozy within, protected by the thickness of its walls from the moist southwesterly winds, or the cold southeasterlies that occasionally swept up the valley.

There was a feeling about the cottage that Matthew enjoyed, a feeling of belonging, a feeling of history perhaps, he admitted to himself. Maybe old Williams was right after all. Maybe history was all around us.

Matthew ran up to the front door, thrust it open, and yelled "I'm back!" at the top of his voice. He crept quietly into the kitchen, drawn by the warm, fresh smell of baking, and before his mother could protest had seized a couple of scones hot from the oven and sweet to the taste.

"Matthew!" his mother exclaimed, wiping floury hands on her apron. "Come back!"

"I'm going to do my homework," he said indistinctly, his mouth filled with a scone.

Astonishment at his reply silenced his mother, and smiling, she returned to her baking, shaking her head at the boisterousness of her twelve-year-old son.

"What will become of him?" she said aloud. "He's as restless as the stream outside."

•2•

THE FOLLOWING DAY, Saturday, was gloriously warm and sunny, a pleasant afterglow of summer, and Matthew took little persuading to go blackberrying.

"And bring back enough for a pie for dinner," said his mother, handing him a bowl. "Don't eat all you pick. The rest of us want some too."

The day was too nice to allow Matthew to be indignant at his mother's suspicions of him. Besides, she was right; it would be easy to linger, eating the black, succulent fruit, and forget the family waiting at home. He knew where the best berries were to be found, hanging in clusters, like grapes almost. He sauntered along the lane to the bushes he knew.

He picked slowly and casually, eating every third berry he picked. That, he thought, was a fair reward for his labor. His lips were soon colored a deep purple from the juice, but his bowl was filling, if slowly.

He stopped as he saw one branch, almost hidden in the thicket, hanging heavy with fruit. He put his bowl down on the grassy bank and reached up to the bough. The fruit was higher than he had thought. It was out

8

of reach, but he was determined, now that he had seen it, to gather it in. He climbed further up the hedge, hardly aware of the thorns scratching at his arms and catching his clothing. He reached up and forward and grabbed at the swinging branch. He could just reach it. He held it between two fingers and pulled it gently toward him. The fruit was so ripe and ready for picking that a sudden movement would set it falling, lost, into the tangle of grass and weeds below.

He inched his fingers cautiously along, stretching out further from the hedge. A flailing bramble, spiny with thorns, caught at his cheek and he turned sharply away, let go of the branch, twisted awkwardly to regain his balance, and fell through the thicket of brambles into a ditch beyond.

He was startled and annoyed. He lay looking up at the tantalizing sway of blackberry-laden boughs above him. The sky beyond was clear blue, with not a wisp of cloud; the lazy buzz of insects hovered about his ears.

Matthew was angry with himself. He put up a hand to his cheek, where the thorns had drawn blood. His bare arms were scratched, too. And the bowl of blackberries was on the other side of the hedge.

He looked about him and realized at last where his scramble over the hedge had brought him. He was in the graveyard. At his feet was a cracked headstone, and as he lay peering through the long uncut grass he could see other headstones, of granite or slate or simple wood, some upright, some leaning crookedly.

He lay for a moment looking at the shadows cast by the bright sun. It was not so frightening a place now, under the clear blue sky, as it had been on his previous visit, when the mist had clung to the trees and lingered about the stones.

Matthew got to his feet and saw that the portion of the graveyard he was in was filled with simple mounds and unelaborate stones, but further on, nearer the church, the monuments were more ostentatious: stone-slabbed vaults, ornately carved headstones, and here and there marble figures.

Where, he wondered, was the stone to the family Mr. Williams had mentioned? Who were they? What was their name? He had forgotten; he would have to look in his homework notebook when he got back home with the blackberries.

The blackberries! He remembered he had left his bowl, only half-filled, on the other side of the hedge. He walked slowly through the lines of graves toward the gate at the bottom of the burial ground. He wanted to hurry to get to his bowl, but it did not seem right to run.

Matthew looked, as he walked, at the carving on the memorials, and paused every now and again to brush moss from the lettering to read it more clearly. There was nothing frightening now about the graveyard and its tombs. But a strange feeling had hold of Matthew, as if he knew the people buried here, as if they were speaking to him, reminding him that they too had once picked blackberries in these lanes, been scratched by straggling brambles, and been warmed by the same gentle September sun.

Matthew stopped and dragged his fingers through his untidy hair. I don't remember ever feeling like this before, he thought. He wanted to whistle defiantly, but though he pursed his lips, only a thin, almost soundless breath came forth.

He turned away from the path that led to the gate and walked over to a simple stone and stood before it. He could not say what had led him here, but he had to linger. He stood looking at the stone, peering to read the lichen-covered carving.

It was very difficult to make out the lettering, but it seemed important to do so. He stretched out a hand to the stone. As he touched it he felt a warm, tingling sensation at the tips of his fingers. Gently he rubbed at the yellow-green lichen and slowly the letters became legible. He sat cross-legged at the foot of the stone and gazed. As he looked, the letters became clearer, the words formed, and the names shaped themselves for him.

TO THE MEMORY OF
REUBEN VISICK, AGED 40, OF GWENNAP,
AND HIS SONS, CHARLES VISICK,
AGED 20, AND JOHN VISICK, AGED 17,
WHO WERE ALL KILLED AT WHEAL MAID
ON JULY 21ST, 1852, AND ARE BURIED HERE.

Matthew paused in his reading, for somehow he did not want to read further. He closed his eyes and put his hand to the ground to raise himself and move away, but he could not. He opened his eyes and unwillingly read what was written below. The lettering was smaller, the carving less deep — almost as if the stone-mason had added it later, as an afterthought — but it was clear and distinct to Matthew, though the grass from the mounds was growing about it and covered the base of the stone. He had no difficulty in reading it. As his eyes scanned the carving he could hear a voice within him, repeating the words:

AND TO JEREMY VISICK, HIS SON,
AGED 12 YEARS, WHOSE BODY STILL LIES
IN WHEAL MAID.

The words echoed in Matthew's mind, almost in his ears. He sat on the mound at the foot of the stone, in-different to the warmth of the day, shivering slightly, blackberries forgotten.

It was the stirring of a gray squirrel that roused him. It came from the edge of the graveyard and paused in front of him, a few yards away, regarding him suspi-ciously. Matthew shook his head and looked about him. He realized time had slipped by and he hurried to the gate, into the lane, and around the corner to where he had left the bowl.

It was still there, not yet full enough to satisfy his

mother. Quickly he gathered more, putting them all in the bowl. His own appetite for the berries seemed to have gone. His mind was not on his task; his reaching for the ripe berries and gathering them was almost automatic, and soon the bowl was full.

He returned home and in silence put the berries on the kitchen table.

"Why, you've been quick!" his mother said.

Matthew was surprised. He thought he had spent a lot of time lingering in the graveyard.

"You look pale," she went on. "And you've scratched yourself all over. Come here, love." She was standing by the kitchen sink and she put her arm round Matthew's shoulder and gently wiped the blood from the scratches on his arms and cheek. "It's not too bad," she said, and kissed him swiftly on the forehead before he could wriggle away.

She looked after him anxiously as he turned away from her and stood at the door, looking in silence at the garden and, beyond, at the trees that hung over the lane.

Matthew was listening. A breeze was playing softly through the leaves and the stream was lapping lazily over the pebbles on its bed. There was a wood pigeon calling from the grove behind the cottage.

But these were not the sounds that Matthew heard. It was the voice from the tombstone that whispered with quiet persistence in his mind: "And to Jeremy

Visick, aged twelve years, whose body still lies in Wheal Maid."

◇◇◇

That afternoon, as they sat outside enjoying the easy warmth of the September day, Mrs. Clemens said to her son, "What's the matter? Are you sickening for something?" She turned to her husband for his opinion. "Don't you think so, Robert?"

Matthew saw his father glance up for a moment, unconcerned. "Too many blackberries." He dismissed his wife's anxieties.

"He hardly ate any of the pie," she countered.

"Because he'd stuffed himself while he was picking them." He returned to his book.

They talk about me as if I weren't here, thought Matthew. But I do feel strange.

He could not have explained what his feelings were. He was restless, as usual, but it was restlessness in his mind. He wanted to do something, had to do something, but he was not sure what. He idly picked a stalk of grass and chewed until it was stringy and he had drawn all the sap from it. He reached out to pick another and saw someone standing in front of him.

"Mary," he said.

"Come on. If you're doing nothing, come for a walk." Mary Thomas looked down on him. "Come on. Don't be lazy." She turned away and he got up and followed her. She was taller than Matthew by an inch, but slender where he was sturdy. He knew she was pretty. The only thing wrong with her was, he thought, that she knew it too. At least at school, when she was with the rest of her class, she seemed aware of it, but here at home, on the farm, she did not seem to care about appearances.

"I thought," said Mary, "we could have a look at that tombstone that Mr. Williams was talking about."

Matthew was silent and Mary looked at him inquiringly.

"What's the matter?"

Matthew glanced back in surprise. "Why?"

Mary shrugged her shoulders. "Nothing." She led the way beside the stream to the point where the road turned right into the village and beyond to the church. Matthew hesitated.

"Come on, lazybones," she called and ran ahead. Matthew followed, running, and suddenly, as he saw her scampering away, the odd feeling that had filled him since the morning left him. He was conscious now of the fresh smells about him, the sun glinting on the water of the stream, the distant sounds of traffic from the main road. He started whistling and hurried after Mary as she disappeared around the bend of the road.

He caught up with her and together they pushed open the heavy cast-iron gates that led to the church. The church, small and low-built, was at the top of a gentle slope. The tombs among which Matthew had wandered in the morning were at the bottom of the slope, down by the stream. Here beside the church, as Matthew had noticed earlier, the tombs were more substantial and opulent. Here, though again they were neglected, were the graves and vaults of families of substance.

"Ugh!" said Mary in pretended horror. "It's creepy, isn't it?" She pointed to a skull carved at the summit of a stone. "And here." She indicated a wide gap between the slabs of a monument. Weeds clung to the stones. "What's inside, I wonder?"

"What do you think?" said Matthew. "Bones, skeletons."

"Don't be horrid," said Mary.

"You asked, didn't you?" Matthew replied. "What do you expect is inside, anyway — treasure?"

"They used to bury helmets and swords and jewels with chiefs in the olden days," argued Mary.

"That was years and years ago, not in — " He stopped to read the date on the monument. "I can't read it," he said, and stepped carefully up to examine the inscription. But before he could find the date, his eye was caught by the name on a tombstone nearby.

"Here it is!" he shouted excitedly, and then dropped his voice and looked around him as if his shout might have roused the dead from their graves to protest at being disturbed. "Here it is," he repeated in a whisper. "The tombstone to the Martins."

He reached down a hand to help Mary scramble up to join him, and they stood, still clasping hands as they read. The letters were of lead set into the stone, and had been made to last.

Mary read aloud, her voice lowered and expressing the sadness she felt as she realized the tragedies the stone reported.

IN LOVING MEMORY OF
JOHN MARTIN
OF TING TANG IN THIS PARISH WHO WAS KILLED
BY AN ACCIDENT IN WHEAL PINK MINE 1ST MAY 1848
AGED 51 YEARS
ALSO OF ANN, WIFE OF
THE ABOVE DIED 26 DEC 1866
AGED 65 YEARS.
ALSO OF PETHERICK CROSSMAN
3RD SON OF THE ABOVE
WHO DIED 1ST JULY 1829
AGED 13 MONTHS
ALSO LAVENIA ANDREW 4TH
DAUGHTER OF THE ABOVE WHO DIED 9TH
NOVEMBER, 1843
AGED 14 MONTHS.
ALSO WILLIAM PETHERICK, 2ND
SON OF THE ABOVE WHO WAS
KILLED BY AN ACCIDENT IN WHEAL JEWEL
MINE 19 DEC 1844
AGED 18 YEARS.
CAPTAIN NICHOLAS ANDREW
THE 5TH SON. DIED 14 FEB 1872
FROM INJURIES RECEIVED IN THE
BOBTAIL MINE, COLORADO AND
WAS THERE INTERRED. AGED 37 YEARS.

ALSO JOHN, ELDEST SON OF THE ABOVE
WHO DIED 5TH JUNE 1876. AGED 51 YEARS.
EDWIN THOMAS, YOUNGEST SON,
WHO DIED 22ND JAN 1878
AGED 33 YEARS.

"Isn't it awful?" she said when she had finished. She would not let go of his hand, though Matthew was beginning to feel embarrassed.

"Awful? Why?"

"It's so sad."

"Yes," he said, thinking of the accidents that had brought death to three of the Martins and, a voice whispered, to the Visicks.

But Mary was thinking of the babies — the little boy, Petherick, and the baby girl, Lavenia. "What happened to the other daughters, I wonder?" she said. "Why aren't they here? Lavenia was the fourth daughter."

"Perhaps they were still alive when this stone was put up, or perhaps they married. That's it," said Matthew. "They got married and they'll be buried with their husbands."

"Let's look," said Mary.

"No. I'm going," said Matthew. "I've had enough of this place for the moment." Part of him wanted to go on looking, but he knew that if he stayed, he would find his way down under the lych-gate to the grave-yard where the Visicks, all except Jeremy, were buried. He was not sure he liked the feeling that swept over

18

him when he thought of them and their accident. He looked back at the Martin stone. Ting Tang, Wheal Pink, Wheal Jewel, he read, and then into his mind came the name Wheal Maid.

"Let's go!" he said suddenly to Mary, and still holding her hand, he dragged her away and out of the churchyard. He felt cold, in spite of the bright sun.

He released his hand from Mary's clasp and ran away up the hill to the village, out of the leafy shade of the tree-lined road into the open. He waited for Mary to catch up with him. She came slowly, thoughtfully, up the hill.

"I know why Mr. Williams wanted you to look at the Martin grave," she announced. "Don't you?"

"I suppose so," said Matthew, but he did not want to talk any longer of tombs and grave inscriptions. "Race you home," he said, and before Mary could turn he ran past her down the hill.

"Cheat," she shouted and ran laughing after him.

·3·

LYING IN HIS BED, Matthew could hear the wind rising. Already the boughs in the trees were stirring and a loose shutter in the outbuilding was banging with irritating irregularity. It was that, he supposed, which had wakened him.

He slipped out of bed and went to the window. He saw a figure moving across the grass and was startled, until he recognized his father collecting the canvas chairs they had left in the garden. He watched as his father disappeared from view to go around to the back of the house. The shutter banged once more and then was silent. Dad must have fastened it.

Matthew wondered what time it was. It could not be very late, he thought, for his father was still dressed. He went back to bed and lay with the blankets clutched around him to shut out the invading wind. But sleep would not come.

He heard his father and mother come upstairs to bed, their low conversation, the noises as each went to the bathroom, and then silence fell inside the house. He still could not sleep. He blamed the wind, for it was getting wilder, but he wondered why it should disturb him tonight, for no storm before had kept him awake for more than a few minutes.

He got up from his bed and again went to the window. The wind was as fierce as he had ever known. The boughs of the elms opposite were creaking and swaying and he heard a loud crack as one gave under the force of the gust. Leaves swept across the garden in a mad flurry and he could see his mother's rose bushes bending and the discarded petals scattering over the border. The moon was full and high, riding among swift, sweeping clouds. Its light cast sharp moving shadows across the countryside. Matthew wished he were good at art; there was a beauty about the silvery rage of the scene that he would have liked to capture. He was suddenly struck with the strangeness that there was in the world about him, that anything so rough as this night and its storm could hold such magic. He knew he would remember this night forever.

He turned his head to look over to the left. There was a moment of calm as he moved; the boughs hung still, the leaves came to rest, and the rose petals on the lawn fluttered and fell and lay quiet in the grass. At that instant he realized that from his window, in a direct line between the hedges and trees, he could see a corner of the graveyard. The moonlight trapped vividly the stone of one of the graves. He recognized it from its shape. It was the stone to the Visicks, father and three sons, killed at Wheal Maid.

As suddenly as the wind had stopped it rose again; the boughs protested and bent, moaning against it. Swift clouds scurried across the moon, and the tombstone was lost in the dark.

Matthew rubbed his eyes. The vision of the stone had been sharp, but as fleeting as a dream. Perhaps it was a dream, perhaps he was really in bed and all of this was imagined. He drew the curtains over the window and went back to bed.

He slept dreamlessly, no longer disturbed by the night's gales, but in the morning evidence of the rough weather was all around the house — broken branches on the grass and in the lanes, and trees stripped clean of leaves.

Matthew when he woke remembered seeing the corner of the graveyard. He went to his window and peered out. It was so; there was a small corner of the burial ground to be seen, and there, too, a gravestone. Again he recognized it as that of the Visicks, but it was not so clear and illuminated as it had been last night, in the bright light of the moon. Matthew saw that it was the storm that had cleared a path for his sight of the graveyard, for a pine tree which stood at the edge of the plot had been stripped by the gale of its lowest branch. Till last night this had hidden the churchyard from view.

Now it was there to be seen whenever he cared to look out. He recognized the stone and remembered what it said. Even from this distance he imagined he could see the inscription well enough to read the final lines: "And to Jeremy Visick, his son, aged twelve years, whose body still lies in Wheal Maid."

◇ ◇ ◇

Mary Thomas was waiting for Matthew at the farm gate on Monday morning to walk with him to the main road where they caught the school bus.

"You remember what Mr. Williams wanted you to do for your homework?" Mary said.

"Of course. You came with me to look for the grave."

"He said to copy what was written, didn't he?" Mary reminded him.

"Bother!" said Matthew, and promptly forgot it as the bus arrived and he saw that Roger Harris was already occupying his own favorite seat at the back. There was a moment's confrontation before a senior boy, angered at their noisy behavior, threatened to report them.

But Mary reminded him again of his homework when they returned home. "Come and do it now," she said. "You'll forget it if you don't do it right away and you'll be in trouble with Mr. Williams tomorrow if you haven't written it out."

Matthew pretended reluctance, but he was interested enough to agree. "I'm going to the graveyard," he called to his mother as he slung his duffel bag through the open door of the cottage.

"Whatever for?" she asked in a puzzled tone, but he had disappeared into the lane. "That boy!" she said.

"You read it to me," said Mary as they stood in front of the Martin stone. "I'll write it as you read it out. Not so quickly," she protested as he began. As he read slowly, at a speed suitable for Mary's neat writing, Matthew began to see why Mr. Williams had told him to study the inscription. He began to calculate from the dates given.

"He must have been born in 1798," he said.

"Who?"

"The father, John Martin. Nelson was alive then."

"Who was king then, I wonder?" said Mary, pausing in her writing. "Go on. What's the next line?"

Matthew read on, but all the time he was wondering about the other things that were happening in the world while John and Ann Martin's ten children (or were there more?) were being born and were dying.

"You're dreaming again," said Mary.

Matthew realized he had stopped dictating to her. He continued until they had reached the end, and Mary, with a pleased look, held her neat copy out to him.

"There," she said. "Mr. Williams will like that."

"He'll know it's not my writing."

"Tell him we did it together. He won't mind."

They stood, silent and awed, looking about them at

the memorials. The storm had reached here too and broken boughs and twigs lay scattered about the tombs. They walked down through the grass toward the stream at the foot of the burial ground. One other stone had collapsed in the winds, to add further to the neglected and ruinous look of the place.

Their steps were taking them slowly and surely to the Visick stone. Matthew found himself moving off the path toward it, but Mary kept on along the narrow graveled way. She turned to see Matthew staring at a small, unimpressive stone.

She called to him, not loudly because of the sadness of the place, and he did not hear. She called again, a little more loudly, but he took no notice. She went back and crossed the grass to stand beside him.

"What's the matter?" she said.

Matthew did not reply at first. "Another miner's stone," he said at last.

Mary peered hard at it. "I can't make it out." She got down closer to look. "To the memory of . . . who?"

"Reuben Visick," said Matthew.

Mary hesitantly read the engraving, pausing every now and then and turning to Matthew for help. "Father and two sons," she said. "All killed. How dreadful!"

"Three sons."

"Two," she asserted. "Charles, aged twenty, and John, aged seventeen."

"And . . ." Matthew paused.

Mary moved the straggling grass from the base of the stone. "There's something else, but I can't read it. It's too faint. There's a letter *J* and . . . It's no use." She stood up. "Come on." She moved back to the path.

Matthew stayed for awhile looking at the inscription. He was surprised Mary couldn't read it, for it was clear enough to him. The letters were faint, it was true, but he could read them. Their sound was clear in his head. "And to Jeremy Visick . . ."

He heard Mary calling from the lane, disturbing his thoughts. He looked up at the hedge. He could see from here the corner of the cottage and the window of his bedroom.

"Matthew," Mary called again. "I'm going. I can't wait for you any longer."

Matthew turned away and followed her.

•4•

MATTHEW TOOK HIS PLACE in Mr. Williams's history class, trying to escape notice by taking a seat at the side. He saw Mary Thomas looking at him, but he ignored her, as he ignored everyone near him. His thoughts were with that other boy of twelve, with Jeremy Visick. He could not help comparing Jeremy's fate with his own, Jeremy lost somewhere in the workings of an old mine while his mother waited vainly for his return. Matthew shivered and then, in his mind, saw the comforting figure of his own mother, busy in her kitchen baking pasties.

"Clemens." An impatient voice broke into his thoughts, and Matthew dragged himself back to the present. "Wake up, boy." He saw Mr. Williams standing beside him, a look of mild annoyance mixed with concern upon his face. "Clemens, your visit to the graveyard and the tombstone I told you about."

He waited for the answer and was about to speak again when Matthew, his voice thin and uncertain, said, "The Visicks, there were four of them."

"The Visicks? Who are they? It was the Martin stone I told you to copy." Williams was irritated. "What's this about the Visicks? The Martins, boy. Get to the matter." He spoke sharply.

Matthew felt his cheeks reddening. He put up a hand to his eyes, almost as if to wipe away a tear, but it was to dispel the mist that was before them.

"Didn't you have time, Clemens?" said Mr. Williams in a milder tone.

Matthew looked at him. He was not quite sure what Williams wanted of him. The Visicks, they were important, not the Martins.

"Well, Clemens?" The voice was kindly but insistent.

"Yes, sir," Matthew spoke at last. "Mary and me, we made a copy."

Williams put out a hand for it and took the paper from him, with Mary's neat writing setting out the lines of the inscription exactly as they had been set into the stone.

"Good," said Williams. "Would you like to read it to us?"

Matthew stood and slowly began to read, his voice gradually becoming strong and filled with meaning, the Visicks for the moment forgotten.

The class was silent as the story of the Martin family unwound until, at the deaths of the babies, Petherick and Lavenia, the girls sighed. Matthew had just read, " 'Also William Petherick, killed by an accident in

Wheal Jewel mine,'" when the bell signaled the end
of the lesson.

"Perfect timing," Williams said to Matthew. "To be
continued in our next class," he announced and dismissed them.

Matthew gathered his books together and, spirits
restored, went bounding into the corridor and down
the stairs.

◆ ◆ ◆

"You've been fighting again," said Susan Clemens
when Matthew arrived home that afternoon. "Look at
your clothes. What am I to do with you?" She reached
out, took Matthew's blazer off him, and examined the
torn pocket. "Roger Harris, I suppose."

Matthew made no comment, but put up a hand carefully to feel the bruise on his cheek.

"Your hands! Look at them!" His mother took hold
of them and turned them over between hers. The
knuckles were scraped and bruised, and dirt clung
to the nails. "Go upstairs and have a good wash. I
don't know what sort of a school that is."

"It wasn't at school," said Matthew.

"You ought to be ashamed of yourself at your age."
But when he had turned away to go upstairs, she
allowed herself a smile.

Matthew ran upstairs, singing gaily; he set the tap
running and gave his fingers a brief contact with the

soap, rinsed them, and studied the result. It satisfied him, even if his mother might be critical. He ran down the stairs and into the kitchen to search for something to eat.

"Leave those cookies alone," his mother called. "You'll spoil your tea."

Matthew crudely sliced a crust from a freshly baked loaf, and calling, "I won't be long," ran out of the cottage door before his mother could stop and inspect him.

He's going to see Mary Thomas, thought Susan with pleasure, but was surprised when she saw her son turn left along the lane. She went down the path and watched him disappear into the churchyard. She shook her head and picked up his blazer, examining the torn pocket with indulgent understanding.

Matthew did not go into the graveyard straight-away, but stopped here and there to pick blackberries. He skirted the edge of the burial ground, walking along by the stream, kicking pebbles into it or throwing twigs and watching them swirl along with the flow. He walked right around outside the church land and the graveyard, past the old, derelict vicarage and the cottages opposite the church. He saw no one he knew, not even a dog or a cat. It was quiet and deserted.

When he came to the lower gate to the churchyard he looked through the iron bars, unwilling at first to enter. The mounds and memorials looked so still and peaceful that it seemed wrong to disturb them, but he no longer felt fearful, as he used to.

He could not resist an urge to push the gate to open it. It creaked noisily as he did so but there was no other sound. Even the distant traffic seemed to be stilled, and the rooks in the treetops had ceased their cawing.

He closed the gate carefully behind him. It creaked again. Then, as silently as he could, he walked over to the Visick stone. He kept off the path because he did not want to disturb the peace with the crunching of gravel underfoot. He went across the grass, and the only sound was the soft swish of the stalks of weeds and fern fronds as he brushed past them.

He came to the Visick stone and stood, a yard or two away, in front of it. His sight seemed to blur on the edge of his vision, so that only the stone was in focus, sharp and clear in a misty frame. He was drawn to it, though he tried to resist moving forward. He was not aware that his feet had moved at all but realized that his hands were resting on the stone, then that he was kneeling before it and with his fingers was tracing the shallow engraved letters at the foot.

The lettering was clear to him; why hadn't Mary heard it too? Heard it?

He could hear the words echoing in his mind clearly, to the exclusion of all other sounds. Why could he hear it? How could he hear it? He was not reading it aloud. Who was speaking? He looked around him in sudden fright. There was no one. With a sharp feeling of terror that only stayed with him an instant, he leapt away from the stone, turned, and ran.

At the gate, as he put his hand on the iron to draw it open, he stopped. Why am I running? he asked himself. There's nothing to be afraid of. He turned around to look back at the stone to the Visick men. There was nothing to be afraid of there. They meant him no harm.

"Where have you been?" his mother asked when he returned.

"Blackberrying."

"You'll have no room for your tea," she said and then smiled to herself. He always had room for more.

She was wrong, she saw later. He merely picked at his food, not even being interested in his favorite scones, honey, and cream. He was silent, too, throughout the meal — preoccupied.

"Come on, love," his mother said. "Eat up."

"I'm not hungry, Mam, really."

But when Mary Thomas arrived with an invitation to go back to the farm with her to see a new calf, he seemed to recover his appetite. He hurriedly spread honey on a couple of scones, piled them with cream, bolted them quickly, and followed Mary out, noisy again and his normal self.

·5·

MATTHEW RELUCTANTLY SETTLED to his geography homework, finished it in a slipshod and halfhearted manner, and half an hour later went to bed willingly, because in bed, if he was careful, he could listen to his radio. When he slept the sound of pop music still filled the room. His mother switched the radio off when she came to check on him, moved the covers over his shoulders, and let her hand rest for a moment on his tousled hair.

"I expect he forgot to brush his teeth," she said to her husband. Then she added, "He's growing up, Robert."

"Good," said Matthew's father. "About time. Perhaps he'll take life a bit more seriously."

Time enough for that, thought Susan, but she did not speak her thoughts aloud.

◇ ◇ ◇

Matthew woke with a feeling that someone had spoken. It was pitch-dark in his room. He thought perhaps

33

he had left his radio on, but it was not that. He lay still, half sitting up, listening intently. There was nothing except, in the distance, the screech of an owl.

He lay back but he was now wide awake and restless. He threw the bedcovers aside and went to the window to open the curtains. Outside it was dark, and only slowly, as he stood, did his eyes begin to make out the lines of trees and hedges. There was a faint glow in the sky, hinting at the lights of Falmouth, southward. He could see the dark shapes of the trees behind the church, but the building itself was lost to sight in the deep shadows.

His eyes moved back from where he knew the church was, down the slope to the lower burial ground. It was dark there too, but he could just make out the avenue of yew trees at the northern edge. He saw a sharp silvery movement, no sooner seen than lost in the dark. He had imagined it, maybe, but it had seemed real and he knew where it was. It was in that corner of the burial ground where the Visicks lay.

He was curious to know what it had been, though he was more than half-convinced he had imagined it. It was a mild night, he knew, for his window was wide open. He put on his sneakers and, not bothering with a bathrobe, stepped quietly out of his room and went downstairs. He knew his father would not hear him, for he could hear him snoring, but his mother might, and Janet, his sister, was always sharp-eared.

But he managed to get downstairs and through the back door without disturbing anyone.

It was dark behind the cottage. He could hear, he thought, something moving in the outbuilding, maybe a field mouse. He could see that the door was slightly open and the interior was a black hole beyond. He turned away from it and, treading warily so as not to waken his parents, went to the front of the house, along the path to the garden gate, over the stream, and into the lane. He turned left toward the church-yard. He jumped at the clutch of a bramble and felt his way to the center of the lane to avoid the hedges and the mist that clung to them.

He did not know whether he could see his way, but his feet felt certain about their tread. He put his hands in front of him from time to time to ward off anything in the way. He was startled by the sudden shriek of an owl, a quick beat of wings, and a short cry of terror from a hedgerow creature. He wished he were back warm in his bed.

The air, he realized now, was not so mild. There was a damp mist hanging by the stream, and a chill had penetrated his pajamas so that he shivered at the cold. But he did not turn back. His steps led him surely and safely to the graveyard gate. To his surprise it was open. He was sure he had closed it earlier, but now it was open and he was glad, for he thought its creaking in the night would have been a sad and ghostly sound.

The place was sad and ghostly enough. There was just sufficient light for the burial mounds to cast gray shadows. The mist here, nearer the stream at the low-lying end of the graveyard, hung closer, and Matthew could feel its wet droplets clinging to his hair. But the mist seemed to make the place lighter so that as he walked slowly forward, the light traveled with him and he could see his way clearly, past the crosses and the granite slabs, to the corner where the Visick stone stood and the Visick men were buried.

Matthew knelt on the grass, as he had done in the afternoon. He was unaware of the damp that crept about him and wrapped itself around him as his fingers felt their way along the lettering at the foot of the slab, hearing distinctly a thin, small voice saying, "And to Jeremy Visick, his son, aged twelve years, whose body still lies in Wheal Maid."

◆ ◆ ◆

Susan Clemens woke to a knocking on her door. She was instantly awake with a feeling of alarm. She turned to rouse her husband but saw him stir and cover his ears with a blanket.

"Who is it?" she said quietly.

The door opened to show a chink of light.

"Mam." It was Janet's voice.

"What's the matter?"

"It's Matthew."

Susan was out of bed now and gathering her dressing gown to her. She left her somnolent husband and joined Janet.

"What about Matthew?"

"He's gone. I heard him go downstairs half an hour ago. I thought he'd gone to get something to eat, but when he didn't come back I got up to look. He's not in his room, nor in the kitchen, nor anywhere that I can see."

"Oh Lord!" said Susan. "Has he run away? What did I do?"

"Don't be silly, Mam. He hasn't run away. His clothes are in his room. He must be in his pajamas."

"Perhaps he's sleepwalking. That could be worse."

"What about Dad?" said Janet. "Shall we wake him?"

"Leave him be. For now anyway. He's only likely to lose his temper."

They put boots over their bare feet and raincoats over their nightclothes and went out into the lane, swinging a powerful light across the hedgerows.

"It's a strange night," said Janet. "There's an odd feel to it."

"There'll be an odd feel to Master Matthew when I catch him, I'll tell you," said Susan, anger protecting her from the alarm that clutched at her.

"Where can he have gone at this hour?"

"He's been acting strange lately, not himself at all," said Susan. "Has he said anything to you?"

"He never tells me anything. I'm only his sister."

They had turned, without plan, along the lane that led to the graveyard.

"The gate to the graveyard's open," said Janet.

"Why would he go there?" asked her mother.

They stepped through into the burial ground reluctantly, Janet clutching her mother's hand. The mist curled about them and the light of the lantern, as Susan swung it, seemed to thrust back at them. As they moved forward, swaying the lamp from side to side, the stones leapt up, the shadows danced and jerked, and mother and daughter felt glad of each other's company.

"There," said Janet suddenly. "Shine the light again, there." She seized her mother's hand and swept the light to where she thought she had seen a figure.

"Matthew!" Susan leapt forward and put her hands down to her son. "He's cold. Oh, my God!" For a moment she had imagined from the cold, clammy feeling of his mist-soaked pajamas that he was dead, but she put her hand to his face and felt the warmth of it. "He's asleep," she said in surprise.

"Don't wake him," said Janet urgently. "We can carry him."

Susan gave the lantern to her daughter, stooped, and gathered Matthew up. It was so long since she had picked him up. He was heavy but she could support him. In his sleep his arms fastened themselves around her neck. She nuzzled his cheek and slowly stood up.

Between them, with many stops, they got him back to the cottage. As they crept upstairs with their burden, exhausted, they could hear the raucous snoring of Robert Clemens.

Susan stripped the damp pajamas from Matthew and gently rubbed him dry and put him back to bed without his ever stirring from his sleep. When Susan, weary almost beyond endurance, stooped to kiss her son, Janet, surprisingly, followed her example. They both stood looking down on him for a moment before returning to their beds.

◇ ◇ ◇

In the morning Matthew seemed none the worse, nor did he comment on his nocturnal visit to the graveyard.

"Are you all right?" his mother asked him at breakfast.

" 'Course I am," he answered through a mouthful of toast. Susan looked at him with concern but she could see no trace of sickness about him. He seemed as robust and lively as ever.

"Are you sure you're all right?" she persisted.

Matthew looked at his mother in exasperation. Of course he was all right. Then he remembered going out in the night. He didn't remember getting back to bed, but he had wakened there in the morning, so he must have found his way back somehow.

Why, he wondered, had he gone to the graveyard?

He could not remember that. He had a moment's unease, but a look at the clock and a sudden realization that he only had three minutes to get to the end of the lane before the school bus arrived drove the thought from his mind. He left hastily, his mother staring anxiously after him.

Robert Clemens exploded with irritation. "Young hoodlum! Did he do his homework last night?" He spoke accusingly to his wife.

"Why didn't you ask him?" Susan replied with unaccustomed asperity.

·6·

"THROW YOURSELF INTO IT," Jos Stevens, P. E. teacher and games coach, urged. His voice carried over the playing fields and invaded the labs and classrooms. "Run, boy, run."

Stevens looked with appreciation at the second-year boys he had; they were a sturdy, vigorous lot. His colleague in the other field did not seem quite so lucky, he noticed.

He looked back at his own group as he heard a yell of triumph. The greens had scored. A young tousle-haired lad lay panting on the ball.

"Well done," said Stevens. "What's your name?"

"Matthew Clemens," the boy answered.

Stevens had noticed young Clemens before, his wild enthusiasm, wanting to be everywhere where the action was.

Matthew enjoyed rugby. He liked the rough-and-tumble of the maul and took pride in the bruises he ended up with. It was fun, but he couldn't see much point in joining in scrum practices or skill training. He hadn't the patience for that.

"Tackle him, boy!" he heard Stevens shout, and he flung himself at the red-shirted lad thundering past him. They fell together heavily, the wind knocked from them both, and the ball fell and bounced away, to be set on by a pack of players.

Matthew lay still while the other boy got up and ran after the retreating play. Matthew, winded but unhurt, it seemed, lay looking at the sky. What was it he had been doing? He found it difficult to think; there was an ache at the back of his head. The sky was hidden as the bulky shape of Mr. Stevens blocked his view, dark and ominous, looking down upon him.

"All right, boy?" The voice came, faint at first, then booming, echoing. "All right, boy? All right, boy?" It seemed to be repeated over and over again.

Matthew sat up, and the stocky form of Mr. Stevens seemed to appear magnified and then to disappear into the distance, only to return again, large and hulking.

Matthew put out a hand to Mr. Stevens and pulled himself up.

"All right?" Stevens said again, this time with more concern. He supported the boy as he slumped for a moment against him. "Bennetts. Come here." Stevens summoned a boy standing on the touchline. "Take Clemens into the changing room. Sit with him. We'll all be in in a few minutes."

42

Matthew turned and walked unsteadily off the field. What had happened? He had scored a try, he thought. When was that? He was hazy and felt slightly sick. But after he had sat down for awhile and had his shower with the rest, he felt like himself again, scrapping with Roger Harris on his way to the next lesson, getting into trouble with Mrs. Franklin in biology, and ending up with an interview with the year head, the teacher in charge of his class, for noisy behavior in the corridors. All in all it had been an enjoyable day, he thought as he left the school bus and walked home with Mary Thomas.

"Come and see the calf," she invited him.

He followed her into the farmyard where Mr. Thomas, her father, was stacking some sacks of meal.

Matthew had never spoken to Mary's father and was slightly uneasy with him; he was so broad and strong and bluff a man. But today he spoke to Matthew.

"Mary tells me you're interested in mining history," he said.

Matthew looked aside at Mary. What had she told him that for?

"You've been looking at the Martin tombstone, I gather. There's a lot of mining history there, and in the rest of the graveyard. Gwennap was a busy place in those days, the most important place in the world for copper. Nowhere else had copper seams like it, and after iron, copper is the most important metal there is to man. Come in here, lad." He took hold

43

of Matthew's shoulder in his thick, strong hand and turned him to the farmhouse. He led Matthew and Mary to a room at the front of the house. The walls were lined with bookshelves, cupboards, and cabinets.

"My treasure-house." He waved a hand in proprietorial pride to take in the room. "Samples of rock from almost every mine within a five-mile radius. Tourmaline from Poldory, redruthite from Ale and Cakes, cassiterite from United." He indicated without stopping each specimen in turn, rattling off their names and the mines where they had been found until Matthew's attention began to wander.

His interest was caught again at the mention of Ting Tang. "Ting Tang?"

"You know it?"

"Only that's where John Martin lived," explained Matthew.

"That's right," said Mary's father. "John Martin who was killed in Wheal Pink. There was a mine once at Ting Tang. Now, that rock is from Wheal Pink, where he was killed. And that copper there is from Wheal Jewel, where his son William Petherick met his death." He looked at the young lad beside him. "Miners had a hard time in those days — the tinners, and the copper miners. There weren't many who lived to be as old as John Martin, it seems."

Matthew began to peer closely at the rocks and the labels glued to each one.

"Looking for something in particular, Matthew?"

44

Matthew was silent for a moment. He would not have told anyone, but Mary's father seemed to have a special feel for miners.

"Have you anything from Wheal Maid?" he asked uncertainly.

"Wheal Maid! I've not heard that name for years. It's forgotten now. It became part of Damsel mine, I reckon. But look here." He bent down and from under one of the cabinets drew out a wooden box piled high with rock specimens. "Look about among those. I wouldn't be surprised if you find something from Wheal Maid there."

Matthew knelt down beside the box. He felt a strange sense of excitement as he touched the rocks, each having its own special form and color and magic. Each had a small paper label glued to it, and written in neat lettering was the type of rock and the place where it had been found.

Matthew felt to the bottom of the box. He knew it would be there, something from Wheal Maid. He felt certain he would recognize it from the touch, whatever it was. His fingers closed over a rock just small enough to fit into his fist: this was it, he knew. He drew it out slowly, almost reverently, and without looking at it handed it to Mr. Thomas.

The farmer was surprised. "You've found it, have you?"

"Is that it?" asked Matthew, now uncertain, as Mr. Thomas turned it over and examined it.

45

"That's it. Wheal Maid, from the one-hundred-and-fifty-fathom level, Pryor's Shaft. Copper. Pure copper, or as pure as was ever mined in Gwennap. Here you are, son. It's yours."

Matthew looked at Mary's father, with his eyes wide open and a glow in them that stirred the farmer.

"It's yours, boy. Take it now, before I change my mind." He thrust it into Matthew's hand and closed the boy's fingers around it. "Now tell me, boy, why Wheal Maid? What makes you interested in that old place, now?"

Again Matthew hesitated to say, but Mr. Thomas had been so kind and seemed to know so much that he felt that if he could tell anyone, it was Mary's father.

"There's a gravestone that mentions it," he said.

"So there is." Mr. Thomas nodded. "I know every miner's stone in that burial ground. So there is, to the . . ." He hesitated.

"To the Visicks," said Matthew.

"That's right, the Visicks. The father and two sons, killed there at Wheal Maid."

"Three sons," corrected Matthew.

"Ah, but the third was never found. He still lies down below, deep at the one-hundred-and-fifty-fathom level, 'tis said, where the accident happened." He looked at Matthew carefully. "How did 'e know, boy?"

"It's on the stone," Matthew replied.

46

"I never knew that," said Mr. Thomas, slowly shaking his head at his own ignorance. " 'Tis queer, too, that. You being so interested in the Visicks, now. Where your house is used to be called Visick's field. I reckon Visick must have built a cottage there. I expect it was lost to the family when he and his three sons died." He paused. "Had your tea yet, Matthew?"

"No, sir," Matthew replied.

"Then run home. Ask your mother if you can have your tea with us, and I'll tell you all about it."

Late into the evening Matthew listened, fascinated, and only occasionally breaking his silence to ask a question, as Mr. Thomas told him and Mary of the risks and rewards of the tributer.

"What's a tributer?" asked Matthew.

"One sort of miner. The miners worked in groups together, called pares. They didn't work for wages as nowadays; they got paid so much — so many shillings, in the old money — for every pound's worth of ore they brought to the surface. They would work for themselves and share among them whatever reward they got. Now, suppose it was Visick's group. I expect Reuben Visick worked in a pare with just his three sons, so that anything they got would be kept in the family. Now, on setting day, when the mine captain offered different pitches for work, Reuben would bid against the other tributers to work a certain part of the mine — a pitch — in a sort of Dutch auction."

He paused to look at the bright, eager face of the boy, taking in every word, and Mary's fond look, proud of her father's special knowledge.

"You see, the mine captain — the boss, I suppose you'd call him — would know all the mine and its workings. He'd know which gave good pickings and which gave poor. If a pitch was rich in copper, he would hope to let it to a pare willing to work for only two or three shillings for each pound's worth they got. He'd let it to the miners willing to work for the least money. Seems strange to us that they should bid against themselves, but I suppose it must have worked. There was always hope of a sturt, you see."

"A sturt?" asked Matthew.

"The miner always hoped he'd strike a rich, unexpected seam, especially if he'd got a pitch at a good price. They called that a sturt. If they were lucky, they might set themselves up for life. Or raise enough to make a go in the New World."

He stopped again as his wife, a round-faced, round-bodied, rosy-cheeked woman, brought in mugs of cocoa for the children.

" 'Tis time you were off home, my dear," she said to Matthew.

"Not yet, please," he said.

"There'll be times enough like this," said Mr. Thomas, "when you can come and look at things. Don't forget your rock."

But Matthew had had it clutched in his hand all

the time that Mr. Thomas had been talking. He looked down at it. It did not look very impressive. It was a reddish color, and where it was cut smooth at the end there was a sheen to it. It came from Wheal Maid, at the one-hundred-and-fifty-fathom level, Mr. Thomas had said.

"Did you get this yourself?" he asked.

The farmer shook his head and laughed. "No, lad. These came from the family of an old miner who lived over to Carharrack, over a hundred years since. He'd worked in all the mines around. He was blinded in a powder accident, they say. His family kept these for years. I bought them from his great-grandson."

"Time to go now," said Mrs. Thomas. "But come back whenever you want."

"He's a good listener," said Mr. Thomas as he watched Matthew walking through the dark along the lane to home.

Matthew held the rock in his hand, moving it about between his fingers and polishing it. It felt special to him, though it did not look at all out of the ordinary. From Wheal Maid it came, where Jeremy Visick had been buried — perhaps from the very point where the accident had happened. The one-hundred-and-fifty-fathom level, Mr. Thomas had said. How deep was that? He remembered that a fathom was six feet. He did the sum in his head. Nine hundred feet. Three hundred yards underground. That was a long way down.

He had reached home while he was calculating; he walked up the path to the back of the house and through the creaking door into the outbuilding and stood there, looking about at the old, stone-walled, dilapidated building.

He could not think why he had come here. He had meant to go in through the kitchen, but without thinking had come in here. The rafters were festooned with cobwebs; there was a smell of mold about the earth floor; there were holes here and there in the rough slate roof. A wall, with a gap for the door, divided the building into two parts, and from one led some rickety and now dangerous wooden steps to an upstairs room, close against the sloping roof. Matthew's father used this for storing old timber against the day, long promised, when maybe he would have the energy to build the family a boat.

Matthew stood looking around him, but it was dark and there was little to be seen. The windows were small and the glass covered with the dust and webs of years. But Matthew did not need to see to know that this had belonged to the Visicks. He could feel it. Neglected and tumbledown though it was now, he could tell it had been built for them. Here they had lived, he knew.

He shifted his foot and it caught a pile of hardboard off-cuts which came tumbling down with a clatter. The noise, sudden, breaking into the peace which had enclosed him, sent a shiver of fright down his back.

He leapt away and knocked over another pile of half-forgotten household relics. He yelled, startled, and scrambled for the doorway. Behind him he heard a scuttling and a sharp squeak. He fell headlong through the doorway, picked himself up, and ran to the kitchen door. He thrust it open and stood inside, panting and white-faced.

"What on earth's the matter?" his mother said as she came hurrying from the living room.

Matthew could not answer for a moment. Then he said, "Nothing. A rat, I think."

"Ugh!" his mother said. "I keep telling your father to do something. Did you have a good time at the Thomases'?"

"Yes," said Matthew. "I've..." He looked at his empty hand. "I've lost something." He turned to the back door.

"You're not going out now."

"But," he said, "Mr. Thomas gave me a piece of rock. I've dropped it somewhere."

"You'll find it in the morning. Now, off to bed with you."

There was no arguing, and distressed though he was at the loss of the stone, Matthew had to go to bed. In spite of his anxiety about the rock and a slight dull ache at the back of his head from his accident at rugby, he was soon asleep.

·7·

HE WOKE TO HEAR the clock in the parlor below chiming the three-quarter hour. A quarter to what, he wondered? It was still deep night, he felt. He was wide awake and he waited until the clock struck again so that he could count the hour. The boom of its chime reverberated as it came to him from downstairs. One, two, three, four.

He remembered the rock. He had dropped it, he realized, during his hasty flight from the outbuilding. He would go now and look for it. He knew where the flashlight was kept, by the kitchen door. If he was careful, no one would hear him.

He put on his slippers and, treading with care, managed to get down the stairs without incident. At the foot of the stairs he almost fell, for he had miscalculated the number of steps, but he caught hold of the handrail in time and steadied himself. He lost a slipper as he stumbled, and his toe stubbed against the doorjamb. It hurt sharply, but he bit back the exclamation of pain that rose to his lips. He sat on the bottom stair and held his bruised toe with one hand while feeling for his lost slipper with the other.

He listened for any sound from upstairs, but all was silent; there was not even the sound of snoring that usually punctuated his father's sleep. It was an enclosing stillness, wrapped around him, shutting out all sounds of life, of people, of now.

He got up, moved through the kitchen door and over the tiled floor unerringly, avoiding the obstacles in his path — chairs, table, waste bin, washing basket, and the rest — and opened the back door. It did not seem to be locked or bolted as usual, nor did it give its customary grating cry, but came silently back, light and unresisting.

Matthew stood at the door. He had forgotten the need for a flashlight, but stood looking out at an unfamiliar scene in a familiar setting. The sky was dark but there was a glimmer of light from the outbuilding and a soft murmur as of voices, though the words were too faint to be distinct. The thin light moved — the flame of a candle, it seemed — and against it could be seen the figure of a man, short of height but broad of shoulder, darkly clad in rough, heavy clothes, carrying in his hand a small, battered tin box.

Matthew stood and watched unsurprised as the man turned back to the building, the cottage, and kissed a woman who was standing, a candlestick in her hand, at the door. From behind her came two more shadowy figures, one as short and broad as the first, the other

53

tall and slender. They too turned to kiss the woman. Their faces were indistinct, but Matthew could see the features of the woman clearly. Where the rest of the group were gray and shadowy black in the dark, her cheeks were creamy white, with a pink bloom upon them; the eyes were large, blue, and ringed with red, for she seemed to have been weeping. As Matthew watched, he saw her bend down and gather to her the last of the figures to issue from the house, a small, tousle-haired boy no bigger than Matthew himself.

Matthew looked at the woman and saw the glistening fall of a tear down her cheek; he looked again at the figure of the boy, and as he did the boy turned to him, looked directly at him, and smiled, white teeth flashing in a plump young face. He held out a hand to Matthew and Matthew put out his hand to the boy. He felt something in his hand, but the touch of the boy had gone, the figures had gone, and the outbuilding was again a derelict near-ruin.

He shook his head against a dull pain that was annoying him. He looked about him. What was he doing at the kitchen door? It was cold, and an early mist had crept from the stream and was swirling about, entering the kitchen and clinging to him. He pushed the door to and shot the bolts to shut out the world outside. He turned to go back upstairs and hit his knee hard against the kitchen table. He put a hand out to steady himself, and as he did, let something fall.

It was the piece of rock from Wheal Maid. He fumbled about on the floor to retrieve it, and as his fingers closed around it the light in the kitchen was switched on. He looked up and saw his father; he caught the sudden change of expression in his father's eyes, from fear to anger.

"You rascal, you! Disturbing us in the middle of the night. I thought it was a burglar! Why, you . . ." Robert Clemens was bereft of words. He glared at his son, unable to summon up enough energy to berate him further. "Get to bed, boy, and I'll deal with you in the morning."

In the morning, however, Matthew was not well. His mother, when she came to wake him, found him pale, listless, and too sick to be interested in breakfast. She persuaded her husband to leave his punishment of Matthew till later. She knew he would have forgotten the cause of it by the evening anyway.

"I'll keep him in bed today. He's not fit to go to school."

Matthew didn't have enough strength to protest. He slept through the morning, heavily and dreamlessly, unaware of the number of times his mother visited him to look with concern upon him.

Then, about midday, he woke with a ravening hunger. "Mam," he shouted. "I want to get up."

Susan Clemens came slowly upstairs and looked with relief at her son.

"You'll stay there."

"I'm hungry."

"Then I'll bring you something. But you'll stay there till I tell you to get up." She knew she would not be able to keep him quiet for long, but at least she would try.

By two-thirty he was becoming impossible in his demands, and she conceded defeat. "All right. You can get up," she said. "But behave yourself. No running about. Get something to read. Find something quiet to do."

"I'll go for a walk," he said when he was dressed.

Susan looked at him with suspicion. "All right, but not far."

"I promise," he said and went. Now that he was up and dressed he did not feel very lively, but he did not wish to walk far anyhow, only to the burial ground and the resting place of the Visicks. He walked the few hundred yards there and was glad it was not farther. He did not know why he should feel so weak, but his legs felt as fragile as dried grass.

He reached the mound and sat at the foot of the stone, with his fingers again at the base, feeling for the shallow carving of the letters. As he felt the words he closed his eyes. This time, as he seemed to hear the words spoken, he saw again, as he dimly remembered from last night, the face of a boy, lips parted, white teeth gleaming. The eyes of the boy were wide open in appeal. His lips were moving, but Matthew could only hear the words of the inscription: "And to Jeremy Visick, his son . . ."

Susan Clemens had watched her son as he had walked slowly along the lane. She saw him turn toward the graveyard and heard the creak of the gate as he swung it open. What fascination did the place have for him? She took off her apron, hung it on the garden gate, and walked along to see if Matthew was all right.

He had left the graveyard gate ajar and she crept through quietly. She sought Matthew among the memorials and saw him, as she and Janet had seen him that night, curled in front of a tombstone. She was tempted to go toward him and pick him up as she had before, but as she watched he stirred and slowly rose. Susan turned quickly and left. She did not want Matthew to know she had been spying on him.

When he returned home ten minutes later, he found his mother at her accustomed place by the kitchen sink.

"All right?" she said.

"All right, Mam."

"Feeling better now?" She could not hide her concern.

" 'Course. I'm hungry."

She was delighted to hear it and offered him some home-baked biscuits, flapjacks rich with honey and oats.

She watched as he munched. "Where did you go?" she asked as casually as she could.

"Just a walk," he answered. "Not far."

Matthew was annoyed that his mother sent him to bed early that evening. "I'm not ill, Mam," he argued, but she was beyond persuasion.

"If you have a day off school you must be ill," she said.

"I'm better now. I want to go to see Mr. Thomas."

"Time enough for that. He's not likely to sell his farm and move away before you're fit again."

Why do grownups always have the last word, he asked himself as he got into bed, and fell asleep before he could find the answer to his question.

"I'm worried about Matthew," said Susan Clemens to her husband later.

"What now?" Robert Clemens unwillingly lowered his newspaper.

She told him of Matthew's visit to the churchyard. Robert dismissed it as of no importance.

"But I didn't tell you. Janet and I found him there one night, after midnight, asleep. At the same place."

"He'll grow out of it," said Robert, and raised his paper again.

"Grow out of what?" said his wife, exasperated.

"Whatever it is," Robert said. "You worry too much about him."

"It seems so morbid. It's not like a young boy to be interested in gravestones or whatever takes him there."

Susan picked up the socks she was darning, and Matthew's father buried his head in his newspaper again.

"And last night," Susan began again. "Why was he downstairs? And he was so pale."

"Something at school worrying him, maybe? Perhaps he's in trouble there," said Robert. "It wouldn't surprise me."

"Yes, perhaps so. We can find out next week at Parents' Evening."

"Not again!" said Robert. "I'm busy next week."

"Every night?"

"What night is it?" he asked.

"What nights are you busy?" she countered.

"All right." He knew when he was beaten, and in truth he would welcome a word with Matthew's teachers. He wasn't sure the boy was as serious about work as he ought to be.

·8·

MATTHEW WAS GLAD he was well enough to go to school on Friday. He would not have admitted it to anyone, even to Mary Thomas, but he did not want to miss Mr. Williams's history lesson. In the end he almost did, for he and Roger Harris got involved in a quarrel at playtime which led to their being sent to the year head for punishment. Luckily she was busy with more pressing affairs.

"I thought you two were friends," she said as she looked down at them.

"We are, really," said Roger. "Most of the time."

"Then behave like it, and tidy yourselves up before you go to your next lesson. Look at you, Clemens. Blazer pocket torn. What will your mother think?"

"She's used to it," Matthew said.

"Then it's time you learned to mend it for yourself. Come to me at twelve o'clock and I'll provide you with needle and thread. Don't forget," she added as she sent them off. "And I shan't let you go till you've made a good job of it."

"We're waiting for you, Clemens," said Mr. Williams when Matthew arrived. "We'll carry on with the story of the Martins and see what else we can get from that tombstone."

In his clear young voice, Matthew read the inscription again to the class.

"Good," said Mr. Williams. "I've had copies of it made, one for each of you. Give them out, Clemens. There's lots of information about the family there — how old they were when they died. You can work out when the mother and father were born. You can guess, maybe, when they were married."

A hand shot up.

"Yes, Roberts."

"It's not all here, sir. It only mentions the fourth daughter."

"And what happened to the fourth son?" said a girl's voice. "He's not mentioned at all."

"Good," said Williams. "That's the sort of question I want you to ask. Work together in pairs. Write out all the information you can get from it, in date order, and write out all the questions about the family that are still unanswered. And then we'll see what we can find out elsewhere. Get to it."

Matthew felt a sense of pride that it was his homework that had set the class off on its work. But he was annoyed that he himself could not feel any serious interest in the Martins. He knew he should be interested and tried to work with John Roberts, his partner, to puzzle out the record and to list all the unanswered questions, but he found himself over and over thinking instead of the Visicks and their fate, their work at Wheal Maid, and their accident.

"I wonder what sort of accident it was that killed William Petherick Martin?" said Roberts.

"I'll put it down as a question to ask," said Matthew.

"And where was Wheal Jewel?"

"I can find that out from Mary Thomas's father."

"And then, what was the accident at Wheal Pink that killed the father? And why did Captain Nicholas Andrew go to America?"

The questions mounted, and around them the buzz of conversation made it clear that the rest of the class was involved in the same quest.

Matthew's mind was only half on the exercise. As Roberts talked and he wrote, he could only picture Jeremy Visick. He had seen him, he knew, but the memory escaped him. But he could not have seen him, for Jeremy had been killed one hundred and thirty years ago. Nevertheless, Matthew had a fleeting glimpse of an encounter with him. How and when? And why? The vision was elusive, but the features of a boy, wide-eyed, round-faced, came and went before him.

"Matthew." He heard John Roberts's voice and felt his hand on his arm. "Read that last sentence."

Matthew picked up the paper and with difficulty focused on his writing. It was scrawly and ill-formed, as if he had written it just before falling asleep, or in some moment of inattention. It was not like his writing at all; it was much larger, and it was misspelled. *"Burryd in weal maid."* He read it aloud.

"What's that?" asked Roberts. "Wheal Maid? There's nothing about Wheal Maid. Who's buried there?"

Matthew stared at the paper, picked up his pen, and scrawled through the rough writing. Roberts looked at him in surprise, but before he could comment Mr. Williams called for the attention of the class and they began to contribute their questions and discuss possible answers together.

"Homework," said Mr. Williams as the lesson drew to its end. The class groaned, as expected. "I want you all to write an account of the life of Ann Martin, the mother, as told by the facts you've got."

"That's not fair!" said Roberts as they left the room. "What's interesting about her life, I ask you?"

"Ten children at least!" said Mary Thomas indignantly, and, turning her back on the boys, she strode haughtily away.

That evening Matthew could not settle down to his homework. After a halfhearted effort to get to grips with it, he gave up and walked along to the Thomases' farm. It wasn't Mary he wanted to see, but her father, to get him to talk about the mines again, and the miners.

Mary's father needed little persuasion. He showed

Matthew to an outbuilding where he kept a collection of miners' tools. He listed them all — the pick and the gad, the sledges and mallets, the crowbars, the tamping bars, the boryers, the shooting needles, the swabs, the sludgers — describing the purpose of each: for driving into rock, for drilling the blast holes, for tamping the powder home, and the rest.

"They were dangerous times," he said. "Many a life was lost setting a charge of powder. I don't know if that was how John Martin lost his life at Wheal Pink."

"Or the Visicks at Wheal Maid?" prompted Matthew.

"To carry off three of them like that and to leave one behind was likely a rock fall, or perhaps a holing into water." He paused thoughtfully.

"Holing into water?" Matthew did not understand.

"'Tis possible to be working underground next to old workings that are flooded. More than one pare was drowned by breaking through rock into flooded workings. I mind . . ." He broke off. "Enough of this gloomy talk, boy. Let's go inside."

He led Matthew into the comfortable farmhouse. Mary was sitting at a table in the living room. She closed her exercise book as Matthew came in.

"I've finished mine," she said smugly.

"What?" asked Matthew.

"The homework for Mr. Williams. A story of Mrs. Martin's life. Like to read it?"

"No," said Matthew swiftly. "I might copy it."

He stayed by the warmth coming from the log fire in the huge fireplace and listened to Mr. Thomas talk of the great days of the Gwennap mines — Wheal Squire, Cupboard Hill, Poldory, Wheal Fortune, Wheal Friendship (the names rolled easily off his tongue), and the rest — when they produced most of the world's copper, until foreign fields were opened and killed Cornish copper mining.

" 'Twas then the Cornish miner went to make his fortune overseas. They took their skill to South America, Australia, North America."

"Captain Nicholas Andrew, killed in Colorado," remembered Matthew.

"That's right," said Mr. Thomas. "Wherever you find a hole in the ground, they do say, there'll be a Cousin Jack at the bottom of it. A Cousin Jack — that's a Cornish miner."

Mrs. Thomas had come in and added, " 'Twas sad for the womenfolk then. There were many left behind while their men went to make their fortune. Some did, more didn't. There was many a woman left at home widowed, or as good as, not knowing what had happened to her man."

"But a lot of women went too," her husband interrupted. "The miners would send money back, bit by bit, to pay passage for their wives and families." He shook his head. "But they were sad, desperate times, for tens of years. First copper died, then tin."

65

"Was it finished, then? Was there no more to be got?" Matthew asked.

"Bless your life, me dear. There's more down there than was ever got up, they do say. But 'tis costly and difficult work to get it. Aye, and still dangerous. Hard-rock mining is full of risk."

Mrs. Thomas smiled at the group asembled round her chimney. "You'll all be needing something to drink now." And she bustled away into the kitchen.

"Where was Wheal Maid?" Matthew said.

"You seem fair mazed with the idea of Wheal Maid," said the farmer. "I don't rightly know. Somewhere between Todpool and Sunny Corner, over that way beyond United Downs. It'll all be lost now, I do reckon. Maybe one or two old shafts about. Don't you go wandering over there, boy. 'Tis too full of holes for safety. 'Tis riddled with shafts."

❖ ❖ ❖

Matthew slept soundly that night, only waking with the feeling that if he could remember his dreams, he would make a discovery. What sort of discovery he did not know, but he felt he was on the edge of uncovering something important, important to him at least. But as he lay drowsing, with the feeling of Saturday-morning leisure to comfort him, he could not, try as he would, recapture the dream. The harder he tried, the more the dream faded, until by the time he got up even the echoes of it had died away and he could not remember having dreamed at all. But he still had a feeling of expectation unfulfilled.

He looked out of the window. It was a bright, clear day, crisp and autumnal, tempting him outside. There would be some chores to do, but once those were finished he would be free.

As soon as he could, he got ready for a long walk. He was mildly annoyed when Mary Thomas arrived. He had wanted to go on his foray alone, but as he looked at her, dressed in jeans and sweater, her long fair hair flowing loosely behind her, he decided he could put up with her company. She wasn't too bad and he had to admit that because of her father, she was likely to know more about mines than he did.

"Be back for lunch, prompt at one o'clock."

Matthew waved in recognition of his mother's reminder and turned left along the lane. Together they walked past the graveyard and beside the stream that ran along its boundary. After a while they came out of the shelter of the trees to more open country, and the land seemed to change.

"United Downs," said Mary.

It was strange, thought Matthew, that he had never been here before. It was only a mile or so from home.

He knew why he had not been here as soon as he and Mary reached the top of the hill. They could see, from where they stood, a desolate landscape pockmarked with old mine workings, sad with the derelict ruins of engine houses, chimney stacks battered by storm but still standing: stone skeletons, sentinels over the land where they had once proudly worked. It was at first sight depressing; man's neglect and contempt for his past (and his scornful treatment of the earth) were evident everywhere. Rubbish was negligently deposited here and there — an old mattress, the decaying body of a motorcar, a pile of empty paint cans. Around one area a line of rusting corrugated iron sheets marked a rudimentary racetrack for stock cars. The once great, prideful copper field of Gwennap was despoiled and despised.

Nature, Matthew saw, had tried to hide the results of man's neglect. Heather grew wherever it could find a hold and was flowering freely.

As Matthew looked, he began to see past the rubble and the idle scatterings of waste and to recognize a majesty about the landscape. Mary was going to walk on, but Matthew paused to scramble up a cluster of rocks to a vantage point.

"Look," he said. "That line of chimneys. Aren't they wonderful? That very tall one, what's that, I wonder?"

Mary joined him and her eyes followed his pointing hand. "Killifreth," she said.

"It's elegant," Matthew said. He was glad now that Mary was with him. He was not afraid of expressing himself freely when she was there. "This near one, what's this?"

"Wheal Clifford, I think. And that's Poldory."

"And whereabouts is Wheal Maid?"

"I don't know if there's a stack or engine house to mark Wheal Maid," Mary replied.

"Come on." Matthew clambered down from the rocks and set off across country, where old paths were faintly marked, crisscrossing the heather. He set a swift pace, as if he knew just where he was going. He had no hesitation when he came to a point where three tracks intersected. He knew without thinking which one to take, and strode on purposefully. He did not stop to wait for Mary and was hardly conscious of her pattering along behind him. He was quite unaware of her protests at the pace he was setting. He did not know when she stopped and left him to go on alone.

He walked a few hundred yards farther and halted. He was not certain why he had stopped. In front of him the ground fell at a fairly sharp incline to a valley. Clumps of heather spangled the slope. Here and there bare rock was revealed, and evidence of old stone walls, rock squared and placed to rim the entrance to a shaft.

As he looked, Matthew was reminded of the warning given by Mary's father about the dangers of the old workings. He peered down the slope and thought that he saw, twenty or thirty yards below, a dark hole, at its mouth a clutter of rocks. He was reminded too of Mr. Thomas's remark that wherever you find a hole in the ground, there's a Cornishman at the bottom of it.

Matthew got down on his knees and was beginning to scramble down among the tumbled rocks and heather when a cry from Mary halted him. She was standing a few yards back, calling to him.

"What's the matter?" he called impatiently.

"No," she said. "You mustn't go. You heard what Dad said. It's dangerous. You'll hurt yourself. Please." Her face was pale and her eyes dark with apprehension.

"What's the matter?" he repeated.

"You mustn't. It isn't safe. Let's go back." She half turned away.

Matthew stood up. Whatever impulse had drawn him here to the edge of the valley had been broken. He looked back down the slope at the rocks and heather; it did look dangerous, he realized. He had no wish now to descend and explore.

"Coming," he shouted and caught up with Mary. They walked slowly home chattering about school and friends.

·9·

MATTHEW WANTED TO HAVE Sunday free, so he settled down to his homework on the evening of Saturday, shutting himself in his bedroom to do it. His French got scant attention; his math he did rapidly, untidily, but correctly; and then he got down to the homework Mr. Williams had given them.

What kind of woman was Ann Martin, wife of the miner John Martin, mother of miners William and Nicholas? He sat and mused, idly looking out of his bedroom window in the direction of the graveyard. He peered out toward the gap in the line of trees and could make out the tombstone.

But it was the tombstone of the Visicks, not the Martins. He tried to drag his mind back to the Martins, to give his attention to the work he had been assigned, but whenever he thought of miners it was Jeremy Visick, young miner of twelve, who came to mind, and when he read of the accidents that had brought death to the Martins his attention immediately shifted to the disaster at Wheal Maid that had brought to Jeremy's mother the loss, at a stroke, of her husband, Reuben, her sons Charles and John, and her youngest boy, Jeremy.

How did he know Jeremy was the youngest boy? He closed his eyes and saw the face of the woman who had stood at the door of her cottage, saying good-by to her mining men as they went to work.

Matthew stayed at the window, motionless, as dark came, his work forgotten, the pen fallen from his hand, and his exercise books ignored.

Below, from the living room, as Matthew walked down the stairs, came the subdued sounds of the television. Matthew walked past into the kitchen and out through the back door.

It was quite dark now and the air hung listless about the shrubs and trees. There seemed to be no stars, and then Matthew realized he was not in the open but was standing in the shadow of the outbuilding wall, inside the building. He could feel the clammy earth floor beneath his bare feet. It was tramped hard with use.

Gradually his eyes became accustomed to the light. He was somehow not surprised to see that the outbuilding was tidy and neat, no lingering cobwebs at the windows, no clutter of garden tools or lumber, but here a deal table, its top scrubbed clean, with two chairs and a bench beside it. On the table was a tin candlestick holding the end of a candle, sputtering and throwing a black smoky plume to the roof. Matthew could smell the tallow.

He wanted to move forward to the woman who sat at the table, head in her hands. She seemed to be staring at him, but if she saw him, it was without interest or recognition. Her eyes were filled with despair. He had seen her before, of course, on his last visit to her cottage. In the light cast by the candle, her cheeks were still creamy white, as they had been, but instead of the pink rose-bloom he had seen before there were gaunt shadows on her cheeks, cast by the flickering candle flame. Her blue eyes now looked dark, large, and tear-filled.

Matthew wanted to reach out to her, but his hands were immovable. The woman got up from the table with a resolute air, as if to dismiss her cares, and went over to the corner of the room. There was a narrow wooden bed and on it slept two young girls clinging to each other. Their mother bent down and pulled a thin blanket over their bare arms. She moved then to the other wall, and Matthew followed her and looked over her shoulder as she stooped over another bed, larger and unoccupied. Matthew knew, as he watched, that this was the bed of her three sons.

She turned away. Matthew felt she would see him and could not fail to touch him, but she walked past without noticing his presence, picked up the candlestick, and went to the corner of the room where the stairs were and climbed slowly up.

Matthew followed. He looked around as the candle, now sputtering to the end of its life, threw uneasy, fitful light over the bare walls. By the small window stood a frail cabinet, upon it a Bible; between the window and the door, almost filling the room, was a bed. Upon the bed, lying close together, were three still figures in torn and stained clothes. Matthew could not tell where the red of the mine dust ended and the red of blood began. He was looking at the bodies of Reuben Visick, stocky and once strong, and of his two older sons, Charles and John.

The woman put the dying candle on the cabinet and turned to go downstairs. Matthew could not get out of her way and stumbled. The rotting steps in the outbuilding gave way and he fell with a clatter to the floor, dislodging an old tin bath that was hanging on the wall. Its metallic clanging echoed about the old building. Matthew lay stunned and bewildered at the foot of the steps.

A light blazed at him. He heard his father's voice, angry and at first incoherent.

"You again! What am I to do with you? Look at the mess you've made. Get up and I'll give you a good thrashing here and now."

"He's hurt," said Matthew's mother. "Can't you see?"

"I'll hurt him," his father said, unreasoningly.

Matthew, dazed and unsure, felt his mother's arm about him. Dizzily he struggled to his feet and said, "Mrs. Visick, is she all right?" and collapsed.

Robert Clemens was immediately contrite and helped his wife carry the boy to bed.

"He looks dreadful," he said. "Perhaps you're right. Maybe he is sickening for something."

While Susan was getting Matthew into bed, her husband tidied the pile of exercise books. He picked up the school copy of the Martin tomb inscription.

"What's this nonsense?" he said. "No wonder the boy's head is filled with morbid rubbish if the school encourages this sort of thing. I'll tell them something when I go to their Parents' Evening."

Susan smiled to herself. Robert always covered up his worries about the children in some display of anger or irritation.

"Yes, dear," she said, and felt Matthew's forehead for signs of fever. As she did, he opened his eyes.

"Well, you gave us a fright," she said.

"And interrupted the film," said his father gruffly.

"I'm sorry," said Matthew. "What happened?"

"You were in the outbuilding. Goodness knows why. And you fell down the steps." His mother looked at him with concern. "Are you all right?"

"Yes," said Matthew. "I guess so." There seemed to be a tender place on his bottom, where he had fallen, but nothing serious.

"I'm all right." But he was not sure he was. Something at the back of his mind was worrying him.

"I'll fetch you a hot drink," said his mother, but when she returned with it, he was asleep.

There seemed to be no aftereffects of the incident, apart from added disorder to the outbuilding. Matthew felt no aches or pains and, though his mother wanted him to stay in bed, he persuaded her to let him up for breakfast. When she asked him to help prepare the vegetables for their Sunday dinner he was glad to be busy and out of his father's way until his temper had been soothed by a long session with the Sunday paper.

Then, in the afternoon, he went with his mother for a walk to her older sister's. He usually disliked having to visit Aunt Mabel's but today he didn't mind. Perhaps his mother was trying to keep him occupied, he thought, so that he wouldn't get into mischief. But she needn't have worried. He wasn't feeling the least bit lively, and the walk passed surprisingly quietly, without incident.

He *is* sickening for something, thought Susan as they returned home. He had eaten hardly anything of the substantial tea Mabel had provided. There must be something amiss. As they walked along she looked out of the corner of her eye at him. He seemed well enough, but by now she would have expected him to be running on ahead, scuffing his shoes against the stones at the roadside or throwing sticks up into the trees; the most unnatural thing was for him to be walking, as he was, sedately by her side.

"He's growing up," she thought sadly.

·10·

WHEN PARENTS' EVENING came Robert did not forget his threat to make an issue over the work Matthew had been given. It did not take him long to discover that it was young George Williams, the history teacher, who had issued copies of the Martin tomb inscription to his class.

"What's this rubbish?" Robert Clemens thrust the copy in front of Williams even before he sat down.

"Robert!" Susan gently protested.

Robert turned to his wife as if to silence her, but she, asserting her authority, turned to the teacher in explanation. "We're worried about Matthew, you see," she said.

Robert, angry that the initiative had been taken from him, sat sulkily with folded arms.

Williams listened as Mrs. Clemens went on.

"Matthew has had one or two strange turns lately. We found him once, in the night, in the churchyard, and twice he's been up, sleepwalking maybe, and doesn't seem to remember what he's been doing. I've seen him going into the graveyard and looking at the stones." She hesitated. "It doesn't seem natural — for a young boy, I mean. And then we found this . . ." She paused and Robert seized his chance.

"That sort of thing! What good is that sort of thing? Filling up his time with nonsense like that! History, is it? It's rubbish, if you ask me."

Williams smiled. "That's what Matthew said."

"Oh, did he? Then he's got more sense than I supposed," said Mr. Clemens.

"I don't think he thinks so now, though. He's done some good work already for me."

"Good work!" Robert was surprised and Susan gratified.

"He's a bright lad. His problem is that he's interested in everything. A good fault, but he's got to learn to concentrate. He's young enough. It will come."

"Young enough! He's twelve," said Robert. "Time he was getting down to work. There was a time when a lad of twelve would be out at work, earning his living."

Williams interrupted. "That's true. Is that what you want for your son, Mr. Clemens? To be out at work at twelve?"

"Well," said Matthew's father uncertainly. "He could take life more seriously."

"Oh, I agree," said Mr. Williams. "Life's a serious business. He's a bit scatterbrained, but he wouldn't be a boy if he weren't."

"This work you gave," Robert shifted his ground. "It's morbid, and it's started Matthew off on morbid fancies."

"Yes," said Williams. "That's strange. The rest of the class have taken it in their stride and done some good essays. It's turned out just as I planned. But I admit, with Matthew it's different somehow. It seems to mean more to him." He took a folder from his desk and produced a sheet of paper.

"Here's Matthew's latest piece of work. The class were asked to put themselves in the place of Ann Martin and to picture things from her point of view." He smiled. "The boys didn't like that, but in the end they turned out some cracking good work. Matthew's was different. Read it. You'll see what I mean." He handed the paper to Matthew's parents and moved away to talk to another couple while Robert and Susan read their son's work.

It was unmistakably Matthew's, thought Susan. The writing was firm and neat and characteristically his at the start, and then, as the interest of the story took over, it became hurried and untidy and blotted. It was brief, but graphic.

The miner's wife stood at the door of the cottage and said good-by to her husband and three sons. They were going to work at the mine, Wheal Maid. It was not yet daylight and she sighed as she saw them disappear in the dark.

79

She turned back into her little house and went over to the truckle bed where her two youngest children, both girls, were sleeping. She thought, "Well, you won't have to go down the mine, I hope," and sat at the table where she dozed till dawn.

When daylight came she got busy about the house. There was not much to do because it was so small. But there were always clothes to mend and water to be carried from the stream, and wood to be collected for the fire.

When she had finished that and got the herring out of the brine to be ready for the men when they came back, she told her two daughters to come with her to meet their father and brothers.

"They will be coming up to grass soon," she said. "It's a nice day. We'll walk to Sunny Corner to meet them."

They set off slowly, because they had plenty of time and it was warm, being summer. The girls skipped ahead. Before they got to Sunny Corner they stopped as a man on horseback came riding toward them. He got down from his horse. His face was serious and he did not speak at once.

"Mrs. Visick," he said at last. "I think you should get back home."

The miner's wife looked hard at him.

"They will be bringing your man and two sons home . . ." He knew she understood. It was not the first time he had had to carry messages like this and he knew it would not be the last.

"Two sons?"

"Charles and John."

"And Jeremy?"

The man shook his head. "He's still below. We cannot bring his body back. He's buried there."

◊ ◊ ◊

The last three words were written and scored through and then rewritten.

Susan looked up at her husband, waiting for him to finish. Mr. Williams was standing by now, waiting for their comments.

"He writes about a Mrs. Visick, you see, not Mrs. Martin. And a disaster at Wheal Maid which killed the husband and three sons. There's nothing like that on the Martin stone."

"It's unhealthy," said Robert, "writing about death like that."

Susan was silent, thinking back to Monday of that week. Matthew had come home from school and, without stopping to make his usual raid on the kitchen, had gone out again. He had come back later, white-faced, and instead of sitting down with the rest of them, had gone up to his room. After a quarter of an hour she had sent Janet to bring him down.

"He's doing his homework," Janet had reported. "I didn't want to interrupt him."

Susan had then gone up herself. Matthew had been writing and, intent on his work, had not noticed her looking over his shoulder. She knew now that this was what he had been writing. She had left him, and when he joined them a few minutes later he had seemed normal enough, noisy and hungry.

"Who is Mrs. Visick?" Williams asked. "Does she mean anything to you?"

"He's got a vivid imagination," Susan said in defense of her son, but she recollected, uneasily, that she had heard him mention the name.

"I wouldn't worry, anyway." Williams tried to reassure them. "He's a bright lad, usually very lively — sometimes too much so. He'll snap out of this mood, I shouldn't wonder." But he resolved to watch Matthew more closely and to have a word with his former tutor. He repeated his assurances. "He'll get over whatever it is soon enough."

"He'd better," said Matthew's father. "He'd better."

◇ ◇ ◇

Matthew, meanwhile, was behaving like his normal self at home. He had developed a fierce hunger for something sweet. He had searched everywhere and found no cookies, no cake, no scones. It was unlike his mother to leave so bare a larder. He decided he would have to make something for himself. Unhappily, he had fooled about in his cooking lessons at school and had only dim memories of the recipes he had been given. His fragmentary notes would be useless. He would have to call on his memory.

Eggs, he supposed; sugar certainly, butter maybe,

and, he thought, flour. He looked through the cupboards — honey, golden syrup, powdered chocolate,
raisins. He chose a large bowl, made a hasty assem-
bly of ingredients, haphazardly measured them, and
stirred them together vigorously with a wooden spoon.

He remembered something about "dropping consistency." He had had fun with that in school; he had
transformed it to "flicking consistency" — firm enough
to hold to the spoon and soft enough to be flicked
across the room. He tried that, without stopping to
think, and a large conglomerate mass of flour, raisins,
eggs, and honey spattered across the kitchen.

Matthew stared in horror and with more haste than
care wiped away the mess, or what he could find of
it. He dipped a finger in the mixture, but the taste
was awful. Still, he was sure it would be better cooked.
He got out a muffin pan and ladled the mixture into
the hollows. He put it in the top oven of the stove.

He took the leftover mixture outside and spent an
interesting few minutes flicking it at the privet hedge
at the side of the garden. It looked as if the hedge
were bearing a strange fruit, globules of sticky mixture clinging to the branches and dripping slowly,
drop by heavy drop, through the leaves.

At that moment the car drew up and his mother
and father appeared. They had driven in thoughtful
silence from the Parents' Evening. Their minds were
full of the contradictory reports they had had of their
son; they all added up in Susan's mind to the fact

that he was boyish, lively, naughty, likable, but changing, growing up, uncertain of himself, moody. To Robert, Matthew seemed to be irresponsible, wild, and lazy: it was no use teachers saying he was a bright lad with plenty of promise if they let him get away with stuff like that Visick nonsense. By the time the couple reached home, Susan was heavy with regret at the thought of losing a boy; Robert was brooding with impatience at his son's childishness — would he never take life seriously?

The sight of Matthew guiltily caught in the glare of the headlights, with the empty mixing bowl in one hand and a wooden spoon in the other, roused Robert to fury. "What the . . . !" he spluttered and leapt from the car. He seized Matthew, dragged him through the house into the kitchen, stared in rage at the mess — the opened cans, the drips of honey, the dough clinging here and there to the cooker. He cuffed Matthew hard about the head, harder than he intended, and Matthew fell to the floor, smashing the bowl as he did.

Robert opened the oven door and was met by the smell of burning sugar. The mixture had oozed over the tray and had spread, brown and cindered, to the oven floor.

"My God!" said Robert. "If I could put you to work I would. They'd teach you in a factory or a garage."

Or down a mine, thought Matthew, looking in dismay and fear at his father. He had never seen him so angry.

His mother took hold of him. "To bed now," she said. "Straightaway."

"I'm hungry," Matthew said without thinking.

At this his father gave a cry of frustrated disbelief and swung out at him again. The blow caught him on the back of the head, and though it did not really hurt, Matthew was so shocked and offended that tears sprang to his eyes. He could not stop his weeping, though his mother tried to comfort him.

An uneasy silence fell over the house as the weeping finally ceased. Robert, morose, guilty, and confused at his own and his son's behavior, could not look at his wife. She had no thought but for Matthew. Janet, aware of the tension, was concerned with her own affairs; she knew her young brother was in trouble, but in a couple of days all would be well again, she was sure.

·II·

MATTHEW KNEW when he awoke that it was the black depth of night, when even the night animals are silent. It's nearly time to get up, he thought, time to be up and dressing for work. Who am I, he wondered? He could not be Matthew, for it was Matthew he was looking at. No, it was not Matthew he was looking at; there was a difference. It was the boy he had seen before, outside, in the night, going to work with his father and brothers. It was that boy. What was his name?

The boy turned and said, quite distinctly, "Jeremy, Jeremy. You know me."

Jeremy was getting ready for work and had put on thick trousers; he was tucking a heavy gray flannel shirt into them. The shirt was too large for him and it flapped about him. There seemed to be enough to clothe two or three such boys.

"It's too big," said Matthew, and was surprised when Jeremy answered, "It's my brother's. Mam's going to make one for me out of it." He added, "You'll need something like this if you're coming down the mine with me." He paused to pick up a canvas bag. It was tied at the neck with string and had his name crudely embroidered upon it. He peered inside it and smiled. "Hoggan for croust in the middle of the core," he said. "You'll need something like that, too."

He stretched his arms and set off, waving to his mother at the window of the cottage. "I'd better be quick or Dad will be out of sight." He ran across the grass, leapt over the stream, and his boots made a clatter as he reached the uneven rocky surface of the lane.

Matthew followed. "You can't come like that," said Jeremy. "You'll catch cold."

Matthew looked down at his thin pajamas and his bare feet. He had not noticed before, but now that Jeremy had spoken he realized how sharp the road was to his feet. He hopped about uncomfortably but ran after Jeremy. He could see him disappearing into the mist. In spite of the jagged stones he ran lightly and caught up with Jeremy before the mist swallowed him up. It stirred and bellied around them, rising dankly from the stream.

Jeremy repeated, "You can't come like that. If you want to come down the mine, you've got to dress like a miner." He strode ahead. They were only a yard or two behind his father and brothers. Matthew could hear the sound of their boots on the road and could occasionally see, as the mist swirled and lifted every now and again, their figures huddled against the night air, the father firm, solid, and small, one son the same, and the other tall and long in the stride.

They seemed to be humming or singing a song together, softly, in gentle harmony. Matthew thought he recognized, from the snatches he heard, a hymn he had heard in chapel. He tried to recall it, but the melody and the words escaped him. He turned to Jeremy to ask him what the hymn was, but the mist had thickened so that Jeremy was no longer to be seen.

Matthew, alarmed at the loneliness which had fallen upon him, called out, "Jeremy! Jeremy!" He waited for a reply, but the mist close about him seemed to thrust the cry back at him. He stood still and listened intently. There came to him, muffled and uncertain in the fog, a faint echo of a hymn and the sound of men walking over the moors to their work and their destiny.

"Jeremy! Jeremy!" he called again, and listened.

This time he heard the boy's voice, from far off, as if called with the hands cupped around the mouth and the words spoken slowly to carry through the night. "You can't come like that," the voice, distant and disembodied, said. "You'll have to dress like a miner."

Matthew looked down at himself. His cotton pajamas were now sodden with damp. He turned for home, but the mist was thick and impenetrable, so that he was afraid and disoriented. He turned again to peer into the gray cloud, but that only seemed to make matters worse. Here and there the cloud turned from gray to black, where the shape of trees loomed, but they gave no clue to his whereabouts. He could hear the water of the stream lapping over its stony bed, but this gave no help either, for he could not tell from the sound which way it was flowing.

He stretched his legs slowly in front of him, feeling his way along the rocky lane. It should not be rocky, he thought. It should be smoothly paved. He felt the sharp prickle of gravel underfoot, clinging to the sole and getting between his toes. He moved with caution, for he had no notion where he might be. He did not think he could have come far, for it did not seem all that long since he had wakened in his own bed. How long had it been? And how had he come here? And where was he?

He was now wide awake and terrified. He last remembered waking in the warmth and security of his own bed, in his own room. What had happened that he was here, and where was he? He knew this was waking reality and no dream, but he tried the ancient remedy and pinched himself to make certain he was awake. He was, and he only really needed the pain of his feet on the gravel to make him sure of it.

He stood still. He dared not move, and yet when he stood still he became more conscious than ever of the cold and damp. He wanted to call out, but did not know what use it would be, or what he could call. Then, without thinking further, he called at the top of his voice, "Help! Dad! Help, please!"

◇ ◇ ◇

Susan Clemens slept restlessly because of her concern for Matthew. She woke several times, imagining she heard noises. Once, as the clock was striking three, she had gotten up to look at Matthew. He had been sleeping soundly enough. She had stood for a moment in his room with him, wanting to reassure him of their love for him, however naughty he might be.

Then later, just before dawn, she had wakened again, uneasy again, and had gone to see her son. His bedclothes were thrust back and the sheets were cold. She rushed to waken Robert. This time he was immediately alert. He too had had a restless night, consumed with worry about the boy.

"What is it?"

"He's gone."

"He can't be far. The kitchen? He said he was hungry." He felt burdened with guilt for the anger of the previous evening.

They looked over the house, woke Janet to help them, but there was no sign of Matthew.

"The graveyard," said Janet. "That's where we found him before. There seems to be something about the place," Janet explained.

"I'll get dressed," said Robert.

"I'll come too," said Susan.

"You get a hot drink ready, and a hot water bottle. You'd be better doing that. Stay with your mother, Janet."

"Robert . . ." Susan began.

"I know," he interrupted. "I'll not be angry. Not with him. I didn't mean all those things." He picked up the large lantern and left the house.

The thin light of dawn was breaking through the fog that clung to the course of the stream. Robert had not been up at this time of the day for years and suddenly, in spite of his worry, felt the magic of the hour. A bird song began, hesitant at first, and then the full fluent cry of a blackbird trilled through the mist. It's going to be a lovely day, thought Robert. Then anxiety about his son overcame him, and his eyes and ears were senseless to all but the need to find Matthew.

He stopped to listen, for behind the bird song he thought he had heard another sound. There was nothing. Even the bird had stopped. He walked on to the iron gate of the churchyard, the gravel crunching underfoot. He stopped again; he had caught a cry, he was sure.

There it came, uncertain, wavering, faint.

"Help, Dad! Please help!"

Robert Clemens felt a surge of affection for his son which swept aside all his impatience of the day before.

"I'm coming, Matt," he called, loud and confident. "Keep shouting so I can find you," he added, for the cry he had heard had been so insubstantial he could not tell where it had come from.

A cry came again, this time stronger. "Dad! Dad!"

"Keep calling."

But instead of calling, Matthew began to sing a comic song that had been a family favorite years before.

My old man's a dustman, he wears a dustman's hat,
He wears gorblimey trousers, and he lives in a council flat.

The sound came, cheerful and strong, in Matthew's lively treble. Robert took up the refrain croakingly and soon they were facing each other, sheepishly singing the song of the dustman.

Robert looked around him. Daylight had broken through, the early sun scattering the lingering mists. He saw they were surrounded by tombstones. His voice faltered and stopped. Matthew stopped too and grinned at his father.

"I don't understand him," Robert said later to Susan. "He was as cheerful as a robin, and as perky. What takes him out there in the middle of the night?"

They knew of no answer. Surprisingly, Matthew seemed none the worse for his escapade and insisted, after a hot bath and a very hearty breakfast, on going to school.

There the day was as usual, a combination of pleasures and annoyances, of pride in being chosen for the under-thirteen rugby team, of irritation at the necessity of turning up for rugby practice because of his selection. But it was a good day, and so were the days that followed, full days that left him happily tired at the end and feeling pleasantly rewarded by the warmth of his home and the affectionate interest of his father in his prowess on the rugby field.

For the moment Matthew had too much to do to think about mines and miners. He threw himself into schoolwork and games to avoid thinking of Wheal Maid and the fate of Jeremy. At times, in the quietness of night he was troubled by thoughts of the Visicks, but he concentrated on other things and tried to put Wheal Maid from his mind. He felt safer that way. The work in the history class had shifted away from the story of the Martins to a look at the local town. Mr. Williams had produced copies of old town maps for his class to study, and Matthew was fascinated by them.

He still walked to and from the school bus with Mary but had seen nothing of her father for a week or two, until one Friday afternoon in early October, as he and Mary walked along the lane from the bus stop, Mr. Thomas appeared at the farm gate.

"Ah, young Matthew," he greeted him. "I've got

something to interest you. I'm busy now, but you come round this evening and I'll show you. 'Tis about Wheal Maid."

Matthew caught his breath. Now that it was mentioned again, he was excited, in a strange, disturbing way. He knew that by ignoring the pull of Wheal Maid he had in some way been disloyal and mean. He did not know how. Now he felt relieved, and especially so, that mention of Wheal Maid had come through someone else. It was not his fault if Wheal Maid and the Visicks had returned to haunt him.

Mr. Thomas was looking at him strangely. "D'you hear, Matthew boy? Come round tonight. All right?"

"All right, Mr. Thomas," he replied, and walked slowly home.

·12·

Susan noticed Matthew's preoccupation during tea. He was quiet and withdrawn. She tried to get him to talk about school but he shrugged his shoulders and was uncommunicative. She hid her concern for him. She had had no cause to worry about him for the past two weeks; he had been his usual wicked self, but here he was, abstracted and remote as he had been when, as she told herself, he had been sleepwalking.

"I'm off to Mary's," he announced. "Mr. Thomas has got something to show me."

Good, Susan thought. They're common-sense people; they won't encourage any fanciful notions.

"I knew Wheal Maid was important in some way," said Mr. Thomas when Matthew arrived at the farmhouse. "But I've been so busy lately I've not had time to look it up. I should have remembered."

"Something about the accident?" said Matthew.

"What accident?" asked Mr. Thomas, puzzled.

"The Visicks, when they were killed."

"Why, no. That was only one of many accidents. No more important than any other."

Except for Jeremy and his family, thought Matthew.

"No. I should have remembered that Wheal Maid was the first mine in Cornwall where James Watt built a steam engine to draw up the copper ore. You know about James Watt, I suppose?" He looked at Matthew doubtfully.

"Of course. Everybody knows about James Watt and steam engines."

"Ah, yes," said Mary's father, smiling at the boy's tone. "But not everyone knows he spent years here in Gwennap supervising the building of his engines. He lived over to Cusgarne. You can still see the house at the top of the village. Well, James Watt built the first steam whim, as they were called down along here, at Wheal Maid in 1784. You mind that, boy. It shows you the importance of Gwennap. You wouldn't think so to look about you now, would you?"

"Is it still there?" asked Matthew.

"Why, no." Mr. Thomas laughed. "The mine closed for a time in 1797 and the engine was sold and taken to a mine to the west somewhere. They never left engines idle for long. They were too valuable. Fine things they were. Noble works of man. And the Cornish engineers better than most. What's more, they gave their engines fine housing, too. And though the engines are gone, the houses are still standing, all about. You'll have seen them."

"Yes," said Matthew. "But not Wheal Maid engine house."

"No," said the farmer. "Not to the best of my knowledge. But the shafts will still be there. I've looked it up."

He put on a pair of steel-rimmed glasses and took up a volume from the clutter on the shelves. "Here we are. There's Tremayne's Shaft, and Champion, and Daw's. And Pryor's, too. That's where that rock of yours comes from. You've got it safe, I do suppose."

Matthew nodded. He took it out of his trouser pocket and held it in his hand.

" 'Tis a pity that old bit of mineral can't talk now. It could maybe tell you tales of the old miners who sought it, could tell you of the work done to bring it to grass. You know what I mean, boy, 'to grass'?"

"To the surface, Mr. Thomas."

"That's right, Matthew. Let me have a look." He held out his great farmer's hand for the piece of rock, and Matthew reluctantly parted with it. It lay, now seeming much smaller, in the large calloused palm.

"What it could tell, Matthew, if it would." He examined the label still glued to the cut face of the rock. "There, see what it says? Pryor's Shaft, at the one-hundred-and-fifty-fathom level. They'd dug down all that way, with blasting and pick and gad, and shifted the rock up in their kibbles, their iron hoisting buckets. Hauled it to surface by the whim. It could tell a tale."

He handed the stone back to Matthew, who enclosed it within his hand.

"I do rattle on, boy." Mr. Thomas looked fondly at the lad.

Matthew sat, eyes closed, hand gripping firmly the piece of rock from one hundred and fifty fathoms down Pryor's Shaft, and listened. The rock was talking to him, it seemed. He shook his head and opened his eyes to see Mary's father gazing at him. He put the stone back in his pocket.

"Where's Mary?" he asked.

"Doing her homework, I reckon," her father said. "She does like to get it out of the way so that she has her weekend free."

Matthew walked home in the fading light. Under the trees the bats were swooping and bending, so swift as almost to be invisible. He walked round to the back of the house and contemplated the outbuilding. There was still light enough to see the clutter inside it, behind the awkwardly hanging door. There was light, but only from the gaping holes in the roof; there was no flicker of candlelight, neither sight nor sound of the family who had once lived there, only the faintest whisper of flight as a bat changed its direction to avoid him.

Matthew turned away in disappointment. Now he knew that what he thought he had seen before was a dream, an illusion. It was lost to him now, all that. The Visicks had gone — father, older sons, and Jeremy. Matthew felt he ought to be glad that he would not be troubled by them again, but he was not. He was desperately miserable; something was unfinished. He had failed in some way.

He did not linger with his family for long. They were all, Mam and Dad and Janet, too, watching television. They hardly noticed him when he called good night and went upstairs to bed.

He took out the stone from Pryor's Shaft and put it on his pillow while he undressed. He would start a collection of rocks. He would need to find somewhere to keep them. He looked around. He would empty the drawer at the bottom of the chest. His mother only kept old clothes there, clothes that needed a patch or were being saved to be sent to a winter jumble sale. She would not mind if he turned them out.

He began to lift the clothes from the drawer. There was an old pair of trousers that he had worn ragged, and an old shirt, torn at the sleeve. He remembered doing that and how cross Mam had been. He turned the drawer up and emptied all the clothes out.

He took hold of his one rock and put it in the drawer. It looked silly on its own. He took it back, put it under his pillow, and piled the clothes back in, all but the trousers and shirt and a pair of sneakers, old, scruffy, but wearable still. He did not know why, but he put these at the bottom of his bed. He had a half-resolution formed in his mind to put them on tomorrow when he got up, to go scrambling among the spoil heaps of the old mines, searching for rocks.

He was asleep before the family came to bed and was unaware of his mother visiting him and tucking the bedclothes tightly around him.

·13·

THERE WAS NO STORM to wake him this night, no bruising pain, no echo of excitement, but he woke again in the dark of night, with the reverberation of the clock chimes still pulsating. He lay for a few moments without moving, only opening his eyes. Once the echoes of the clock had died, there was no sound in the rest of the house, nor outside. When he got up he walked carefully so that he too should make no sound to disturb the family. He reached for the old clothes he had set aside and put them on. He put the rock in his pocket. He was sorry that he did not have a stout old pair of boots to wear, but the sneakers would do.

He stopped as he was drawing the laces tight. Would do for what? Then he recalled clearly, as if it were there in the bedroom, Jeremy Visick's voice: "You can't come like that. You'll have to dress like a miner." Perhaps they would not notice his footwear.

He crept downstairs. Again he did not know why he was being so careful. He knew his parents and

Janet would not hear him; after all, they were not disturbed by the noises he could hear coming from the outbuilding.

He stepped out of the kitchen and stood, his back to the outside door, looking at the building. It was as he had seen it before, neat and trim. Jeremy's father was just leaving. His coat, thick and warm, was stained red with dust; around his waist was a belt, and attached to it were a number of small tools of some kind. Two yellow candles were hanging from the buttonholes of his jacket. Behind him Matthew could see the curling smoky flame of a candle held aloft by Mrs. Visick. The flame revealed plainly the sadness in her deep eyes. She knew what was to happen to her men, it seemed.

She looked at Matthew as he stood there and spoke to her husband. " 'Tes not proper for one so young to be going below."

Reuben Visick replied scornfully, "Don't talk so foolish. He's not young, mebbe eleven or twelve. He do belong to learn his craft, like me and John and Charles here."

Matthew felt a hand at his elbow. It was Jeremy. "You be dressed proper now, except for they pumps on your feet. But they'll do."

The Visick men were kissed in turn by Mrs. Visick. Matthew thought he felt a light brush of lips upon his cheek as he turned to follow Jeremy. He put his hand up to feel; it was moist. He glanced back at the figure of the woman, the miner's wife, standing at the door of the cottage. She had dowsed the candle, for, Matthew realized, candles were costly, and here in this bare home there was no money to spare for needless light. He waved, and though it was too dark to be sure, he thought she raised her hand in reply.

She and the cottage were lost to sight. Once again the mist hung along the stream so that the figures of Reuben Visick and his older sons were but gray, bulky shapes in front of them. But Jeremy was here beside him, cheerful and, in spite of the early hour, wide awake.

"It's early to start work," said Matthew. He wondered if Jeremy would hear him.

"There's almost an hour's walk to the workings," Jeremy said. "First core starts work below at six."

Matthew, his sneakered feet silent on the road, walked on beside Jeremy, whose boots clattered loudly. The mist seemed to be lifting and the figures ahead were taking a less unearthly, a less shifting shape. He could see the tools swinging at Reuben Visick's belt, he could hear them talking, and then he heard one of them — the taller of the sons, he thought — start the melody of a hymn in a clear tenor, to be joined shortly by the ringing bass of his father and the warm baritone of his brother. It was a hymn he recognized again, though the tune seemed more complex, fuller of harmonies, than the one he had heard in chapel.

Christ, whose glory fills the skies,
Dayspring from on high be near,
Daystar in my heart appear.

The words rang clearly back. "Dark and cheerless is the morn," the men sang softly, and Matthew was conscious of the enfolding dark, the glitter of stars, the sharp, crisp feel of night. He could smell the sweet honey scent of the flowering gorse, though he could not see it.

Other smells now began to pervade the air as they drew nearer the mine workings — a sooty, sulfurous smell, and sounds too, of tramping feet. Parties of miners, most of them singing softly, were coming along the lanes, boots clanging on the stony paths, converging on the road that led up to the Downs. There was little conversation between the men as they walked — a nod of greeting, an inquiry about an acquaintance, but otherwise nothing. Jeremy was silent too, but as Matthew realized where they were and saw spreading before him the busy life of the Gwennap copper field, he himself could not keep silent.

"They're working!" he exclaimed. "The engines. The engine houses." There were no ruins to meet his sight, but engine houses: some new, with squared granite cornerstones fresh, it seemed, from the quarry; some old but well maintained; and all supporting the huge and powerful bobs of the steam engines. The bobs, like great birds of prey, hung perched out of the houses, then plunged, hesitated, soared again, poised, and plunged again. Hissing and steaming, thumping and ringing, the mighty engines rhythmically performed their duty.

The chains of the whims, drawing the ore from the mine below to the surface, rattled and clanged and echoed. The men too were noisier as they walked along, parties breaking up as some disappeared into one mine entrance, some into another.

"Britannia, Ale and Cakes, United, Poldory, Consols, Wheal Virgin, Wheal Fortune, Poldice, and Clifford, all hereabouts," said Jeremy, naming the entrances, "and more."

Indeed, wherever he looked Matthew saw the copper mines at work, the headgear above the shafts silhouetted against the sky, the glimmering lights from the engine house windows, the flickering of candle lanterns moving across the workings, the glare from the doors of the boilers, and the dull red glow of the heaped churks or cinders thrown beside them. He could feel the heat from one such pile as they passed, and smell the sharp fumes from the dying coal.

Where it had been silent only a moment before, it seemed now that all was fury — the thudding of machinery, the creak of wheals, the shouting of men, the clatter of horses' hoofs. It was a throb of activity, stirring and hopeful, everywhere. As they crossed the Downs to their own destination, Wheal Maid, it seemed as if every foot of land was being worked —

shafts sunk, timbers framed above them to support machinery — in search of the elusive copper.

Matthew felt his head throbbing with the noise that surrounded him. The acrid fumes hurt his nostrils and caught at his throat. He looked at Jeremy for reassurance but Jeremy had turned away and was walking toward a low stone-built shed. Matthew, his eyes watering and his ears deafened, watched as Jeremy and his father and brothers were handed tools by a man at the shed. They took some candles too, while another man, sitting nearby, made a note in a book as the Visicks moved away.

"Powder?" called the storeman after Reuben.

Reuben shook his head. "I've enough," he replied. "Come along," he said gruffly to his sons. "There's no time to waste. Cap'n Vincent's around."

Matthew saw a man, white-coated and wearing a hard black hat, standing by a long granite-faced building. The light from the oil lamp set above the door shone on features hard with authority.

"That's Cap'n Vincent," said Jeremy under his breath. Matthew felt Jeremy's hand on his arm and followed him over a rough pile of stones, along a narrow path, to one of the timber frames he had seen. Here the Visicks stopped and waited as other groups of miners in front of them lowered themselves into the shaft. Matthew, who could not see clearly what was happening, hung back uncertainly behind Jeremy.

He saw Jeremy's father, who like the other men was wearing a small kind of skullcap and carrying a hardened felt hat, take one of the candles from his jacket and attach it to the hat with a lump of clay. One of the miners waiting to descend passed him a spill lighted at his own candle, and Reuben lit his. The other Visicks followed suit in attaching candles to the clay sockets they had fashioned on their hats, but Matthew noticed they did not yet light their candles. They drew near the top of the shaft as the last of the other miners stepped down and disappeared from view; the thin glimmer of light from his candle receded, and except for the candle flicker on Reuben's hat, darkness fell about the rim of the shaft.

The Visicks approached the hole, Matthew with Jeremy. The shaft was a square of blackness, forbiddingly dark, about six feet wide. Reuben Visick, tools swinging at his belt, stepped down. The light from his candle showed the narrow frame of a ladder against the wall of the shaft, descending deeply into the hole. He moved down rapidly, incautiously it seemed, his hands clinging to the uprights of the ladder. He had gone and the flicker of his candle had gone with him.

John followed his father quickly, and Charles too, till only Jeremy and Matthew remained at the top of the shaft, looking down to the faint twinkle of light that showed in the narrowing abyss. Jeremy stepped confidently into the dark, his feet landing firmly on the rung and his hands sliding down the staves, and moved swiftly down the ladderway. He paused after a few feet and looked up at Matthew.

Matthew could just see his pale face, dark hair escaping from beneath his hat, wet with the night's dampness. His dark eyes looked directly at Matthew.

"You now," he heard him say. "You now." His voice was imploring, insistent, so that Matthew, without thinking and unable to resist, stepped to the ladder, put one foot down and then the other. But as the blackness of the hole surrounded him, panic seized him; he thrust upward, reaching for the top of the shaft, snatched at the stone rim, and pulled himself out. He dared not turn to look, but he heard the voice of Jeremy, fading and echoing about the shaft and finally vanishing thinly below.

"There's nothing to be afraid of," he heard, and then, so faintly as to be almost lost in the dark, "You'll be all right . . . all right . . . all right."

Matthew clutched at the sparse grass about the shaft head, retched with fear, and swallowed sharply, a bitter-tasting gulp. He wanted to cry but swept the rising tears from his eyes with his sleeve. He rose to his feet, and mindless of what was about him — the roughness of the rocks, the gaping holes of the workings, the piled ruins of machinery — he ran.

He was terrified; but worse than terrified, he was ashamed of his terror. He was a coward. He had been afraid to go with Jeremy and he had mistrusted him; he had denied him.

His feet kept running. Warmth was coming back to him as he ran. The shivering cold of the night damp and of his fear was going from him. He saw that the sky was lightening and that life was stirring. A cat, poised hunting beside the heather-covered rocks, was ginger and white; the black and gray of night was yielding to colored daylight.

He ran on and recognized where he was, at the junction of Sunny Corner and the Downs. He looked back over his shoulder before he turned for home. There, against the skyline, were the gaunt, ivy-clung, rook-haunted ruins of the engine house of Poldory. Behind it all was silence, save for the first stirring of the birds and far, far in the distance the sounds of the first train of the day crossing the viaduct over Carnon Vale.

It was his own world again, his own time. He sped on, anxious now to get home before anybody woke. Fortunately it was Saturday and no one stirred early. He ran, panting from exertion, not caring that the dew was soaking his sneakers nor that the brambles were catching at his shirt. He ran past the graveyard and over the stream to home. The sun, still low in the east, just touched the top of the chimney of their house. It looked solid, safe, and warm, and — luckily — asleep.

He crept around the back of the house. The outbuilding door hung loosely and crazily. He opened the kitchen door as quietly as he could and felt immediately the welcome warmth of the stove. But he dared not linger. He slipped soundlessly upstairs, undressed, climbed into bed, pulled the covers over him, and slept.

·14·

By ten o'clock in the morning his mother was becoming annoyed at his laziness.

"It's time you were up," she called, but got no answer. She went upstairs and thrust open his bedroom door. He was lying soundly asleep; his face had smears of dirt across it, and there was a dusty look about his hair.

What has he been doing? she wondered. She looked at the clothes he had discarded: the old trousers, the torn shirt, the ancient sneakers. She picked them up; the shoes were damp and the trousers and shirt had streaks of mud on them. They had been clean when she had put them away and she was puzzled.

She put them aside to be washed again, though they were hardly worth it, she thought, and stooped to shake Matthew by the shoulder. She hesitated; he looked so peaceful and calm. She would leave him a little longer. She knew she spoiled him, Robert and Janet often told her so. She was half-ashamed of her indulgence to the boy, but he would be a boy only a little longer. Time passed quickly.

When eventually he got up, Matthew was quiet. Susan questioned him about the old clothes but he could not explain why they were dirty. She shrugged her shoulders. She had given up expecting too much sense from him.

In the afternoon he sought out Mary and played about the farm. There was always something to occupy attention there, and time passed easily and happily. Matthew did not want to stop and think. There were other things he did not want to do either. When Mary suggested they go to the graveyard to search for other interesting memorials, he resisted.

"I thought you liked going there," Mary accused.

"Not now," he said. "Not now." He knew he could not bear to look at the Visick stone. Even now, in the warmth and smell of the cow barn, he could see Mrs. Visick's face and hear Jeremy's voice. He didn't dare to return to the graveyard; he would be drawn to the Visick stone and then he did not know what would happen. "Not now. Maybe another time." He was shamefaced about his refusal. It was that he was disappointing not Mary, but Jeremy.

When Mary, in a huff, went off to the churchyard by herself, Matthew went home and sat, mindlessly watching sports on television.

The next day he surprised his mother by volunteering to help in the garden, in the kitchen, tidying his bedroom, anything to keep himself busy. He went unprotestingly on the Sunday visit to Aunt Mabel's, and on their return home joined the family in watching programs he usually scorned.

He did his homework conscientiously. That finished, he was reluctant to go to bed. His mother was touched that he wanted to stay with the family and allowed him to remain, curled in an armchair, until he fell asleep. Robert carried him upstairs and Susan undressed him and put him to bed, so gently that, though he stirred slightly and muttered something, he remained sleeping.

The busy hours at school in the days that followed soon made the memories of Jeremy Visick fade. The usual troubles and triumphs succeeded each other. Matthew visited a neighboring school, playing for the under-thirteen rugby team, and according to Mr. Stevens distinguished himself. "We'll have you playing for the Barbarians one day," he said. Matthew did not understand but recognized the favorable tone.

There was only one unhappy note to the days. Sandy Curnow, a large fourth-year boy, had been teasing John Roberts, Matthew's working partner in history. John was small and slight and serious. He had few friends, and though Matthew thought of him as a friend, he did not play with John at school. More robust, active companions like Roger Harris were more fun at playtime. John Roberts would avoid the

rough-and-tumble of the playground if he could, stay-
ing on the fringe of the swirling mass, keeping near
the door into school, trying not to draw attention to
himself, and remaining near the protection of one of
the teachers on duty. He hated crowds.

Sandy Curnow was a thoughtless, overactive ruf-
fian. Whenever he joined the football kick-abouts, he
would kick the hardest, run the fastest, and cover
more ground than anyone else. He did not mind
whose game he joined or interfered with. He would
"borrow" the younger boys' football, run with it for
minutes, then kick it away and set off into another
crowd.

Matthew disliked him. He also avoided him. When
he saw him one morning kicking a ball hard at John
Roberts, time and time again until John ran for cover,
Matthew got wild. At that moment the bell rang for
the start of school and Matthew went in, the incident
forgotten.

At lunch playtime, however, Sandy Curnow again
pestered and bullied John Roberts to tears. Matthew
saw only the end of the affair when John, weeping,
was being mocked by the fourth-year boy. Matthew
could not restrain himself. He ran, from three or four
yards away, head bent, and caught Curnow in the
middle of the back. They both sprawled to the ground
with Matthew on top and Curnow, bemused and
winded, inert underneath.

"Leave him alone," yelled Matthew.

Curnow heaved the younger boy off and slowly got to his feet. Matthew knelt, blood still tingling with rage, quite unconcerned at the consequences of getting into a scrap with the bigger boy. Curnow seemed surprised at the size of the attacker. Then he smiled and came forward. Matthew again took him by surprise when he suddenly leapt from his crouching position and, arms flailing, knocked him to the ground again.

The fracas had drawn a crowd of boys, the younger ones cheering for Matthew and some of the fourth-year boys advising Curnow to cool it, but none interfering. John Roberts, pale and anxious, slipped out of the crowd and went to find a master.

The subsequent interview with authority was unpleasant. Curnow came out of the headmaster's room pale-faced and chastened. He grinned ruefully at Matthew, still waiting outside, and whispered as he went by, "He's in a terrible mood. Watch it." But he evidently bore Matthew no malice.

"Now, Clemens," a voice boomed from within, and Matthew tremblingly entered. He had been in trouble before, of course, but never seriously enough to see Mr. Brunskill. He stood, small and uncertain, in the large room. In front of him, on the other side of a huge desk, sat the awesome figure of the head, remote and forbidding.

"Clemens," said the voice.

"Sir," said Matthew, his mouth dry, his voice high.

Brunskill looked up. After dealing with Curnow, whose reputation he knew, he had expected to find a boy at least six inches taller and twenty-five pounds heavier than this one. What was Matthew doing fighting with Curnow?

"You should pick someone your own size to fight with," he said dryly.

"Sir?"

"What have you to say for yourself?"

"Nothing, sir." Matthew did not know how to explain his behavior. He had almost forgotten that it was his concern for John Roberts, his friend, that had triggered it off.

"Nothing? Then I'll have to rely on Curnow's word, shan't I? It's a good thing he told me the whole story. In the end, that is," he added without smiling. "With a little persuasion." The headmaster looked at Matthew; a bruise was beginning to develop under the boy's left eye, his knuckles were red and grazed, his blazer pocket was torn.

"You look a mess, Clemens."

Matthew was still uneasy. Why was the headmaster dragging things out? Let him get the punishment over with, whatever it was.

"Sit down, Clemens." Mr. Brunskill clasped his hands together in front of him and looked across the width of the desk at the young boy. His name had been brought up before, he recollected. Both Williams and Stevens had spoken in praise of him, one of his imaginative talent, the other of his courage on the rugby field.

"Well, Clemens, I hope you will pay heed to what I am going to say." He waited for a confirmatory murmur. "First, we don't like fights. They disorganize things, distress parents, and don't settle anything. They're noisy, brutal, and senseless." He looked again at Matthew. Matthew nodded in quick agreement.

"I know what made you lose your temper — loyalty. Loyalty to a friend, concern for someone weaker than you. Curnow told me. He took the blame. But . . . he couldn't take the blame for your losing your temper. That was your fault. You won't protect friends by losing your temper. There are other tests of loyalty."

"Sir," said Matthew, only half understanding.

"Loyalty and trust between friends is one of the finest things there is, Clemens, but there are ways . . ." His voice petered out. "Go on, Clemens. Think yourself lucky. Off you go. Tell your next teacher why you're late. Say you've got to make up what you've missed."

Matthew was at the door and in the corridor before the head could change his mind.

On the way home he remembered what old Brunskill had spoken of, "loyalty and trust between friends." He thought of Jeremy. Was not Jeremy a friend and had he not somehow betrayed Jeremy's trust? There was something Jeremy wanted of him, he knew, some reason Jeremy wanted him to follow them down the mine, and he was afraid to go. He was denying loyalty, refusing trust, betraying friendship. He was afraid to follow where Jeremy led.

·15·

HE WOULD NOT go to sleep, though he had pretended to be fast asleep when his mother had peeped into his room. He hoped he had deceived her by his deep, rhythmical breathing. He had felt her warm breath as she had stooped over him to tuck him up, and had thought then that she suspected he was faking, but she gave no sign and in a moment he heard the door close and her footsteps go to the bathroom.

His mind was clear and resolved. He would stay awake until he began to hear stirrings from the cottage at the back. He had no doubt he would hear the family moving to get the men off to work, at half past four or thereabouts. He would stay awake; there would be no difficulty about that. He had never felt less like sleeping.

He heard his father come to bed, and later the sound of a car and muffled voices and snickers as Janet's boyfriend brought her home. He heard the car drive away, Janet creep upstairs, and the clock strike twelve. He heard the clock's quarter-, half-, and three-quarter-hour chimes, then the dull trembling as it struck one. He began to feel slightly weary, his eyelids drooping, though he tried to concentrate on the light at the windowpane to keep him alert. He began to recite French verbs, then nursery rhymes, then to make up rhymes of his own. He heard the clock again. He must have missed the intervening chimes — he was sure he hadn't slept — but the clock had struck three. He began again with the French verbs, but fell asleep repeating, "*je suis*, I am, *je suis*, I am."

The reverberations of the clock striking the hour woke him. It was five o'clock, he was certain. He had counted the first three strokes in his sleep; the two he had heard just now made five. He jumped from the bed, heedless of the noise he made, and hurriedly pulled on the old trousers and shirt which he had again set apart for this. This time, however, he wore his school shoes. They were stout, better than sneakers for working underground.

He looked out of his window. It was still dark. Cautiously he opened his bedroom door, wondering if his parents might have heard him getting out of bed. He pulled it closed after him and stood, his back to it, waiting. There was no sound from his parents' room. That, he thought, was a bad sign. Usually his father's sleep was marked by snores. Now there was nothing. He crept to the door of their room and listened. He could hear faint gurgly noises. Satisfied, he crept away, passed Janet's door with anxiety, and reached the top of the stairs without mishap.

He was impatient at the need for caution. He knew he had missed the Visicks. They would have set off already on their way and be on the Downs by now. He realized when halfway down the stairs that he had left behind his copper stone from Pryor's Shaft. He half turned to go back for it and then decided against it. He needed no mascot or magic talisman.

He was at the foot of the stairs when he heard someone stirring above. He hunched back against the wall. It was Janet. Surely she had not heard him.

He heard her feet pattering along the landing, then the bathroom door opened and closed. He waited awhile; then, when he heard the clank of the toilet chain and the flush of water, he hastened on. He knew that the noises from the bathroom — the groanings of the old cistern, the burblings of the pipes — would hide any noise from him for a few minutes.

He reached the kitchen door quickly, and as he drew the bolts and opened the outside door he heard Janet coming downstairs. He slipped out and closed the door behind him, noiselessly he hoped, and stood, back to the outside wall, breathless. He shrank back as Janet switched on the kitchen light and the glare swept through the window and lit up the outbuilding. Unless she leaned out of the window she would not see him. He heard her go to the refrigerator and take out something — a bottle of milk, he supposed — pour something, and close the refrigerator again. Then the kitchen light was switched off. He moved quickly but halted sharply when the light went on once more.

He heard Janet at the back door and held his breath, afraid she had heard him. But instead, she was shooting the bolts into place and clicking her tongue at the carelessness that had left the house insecure. Then the light was extinguished again, and silence and darkness surrounded him.

I can't get back in now, he thought, even if I want to.

He didn't want to. His resolve was firm.

The outbuilding door swung as he reached over to it. He peered inside. There was the same musty smell that always met him in the building. It was the outbuilding, no longer the cottage, the Visick's home. He felt they had gone and would never return. He had missed the men. They had left. They had all left. He was confused and anxious.

Then, above the earthy smell of the floor, he caught the smell of tallow, drifting, left by the candle lit by Mrs. Visick to see her men off to work. He had missed them, but they could not have been gone long.

He went as quietly as he could across the lawn to the lane. He looked back at the cottage, his cottage, the Clemens home; it was there, comfortable, its vine-covered walls firm and secure. He turned his back on it and ran as fast as he could along the lane.

Though it was dark he did not stumble as he ran, for he seemed to be able to see the path stretching out clearly in front of him, as if he had infrared vision, he thought.

When he reached the junction of the Downs and Sunny Corner he paused, surprised, for he had expected to hear the sounds of the mines at work and to see miners gathering at the shaft heads. There was no one, no one under the vast clear sky and nothing but gaunt empty ruins and heather-covered heaps of dead rock. He stared, anxious and upset. He was too late, too late to find Jeremy and too late to do whatever it was Jeremy wanted of him.

He ran on nevertheless, panting now from the exertion. He turned the corner by the wagon track, leaving the derelict engine house of Poldory behind him, and his heart leapt for a moment. He saw lights at the building Jeremy had pointed out to him as the Miners' Arms, the inn; and there were figures moving against the wall.

Even as he looked disappointment overcame him. It was not the Miners' Arms, though the building was the same; it was a farm now, and the shadowy figures were those of farm workers, making an early start to tend the beasts.

Matthew left the farm behind him. The Downs were desolate, with no further signs of life. Then, in the distance across the heather, he caught a brief flicker of light, so faint and fleeting that he wondered if he had imagined it. No, it had been the light from a candle lantern. He hastened on, leaving the path and crossing the Downs, leaping the tufts of heather, mindless of the pitfalls in his way.

Then he saw Jeremy, standing waiting for him at the head of the shaft. From around him Matthew could hear the sounds of Wheal Maid at work, the clanking of chains hauling the kibbles of ore to grass, the steady plunging and sucking of the pumps, the hesitation as the bob of the engine reached the peak of its swing.

Jeremy was waving to him to hurry, and as Matthew arrived at the top of the shaft he saw Jeremy's helmet moving down. This time his candle was lit and its flame threw a hesitant and unsteady light on the stone walls of the shaft, close and damp, and revealed the wooden ladderway down which the miners climbed to work.

Matthew delayed, a sick feeling in his stomach at the unknown depths of the hole. He would have turned and fled for a second time had not Jeremy looked up and said, his thin voice transformed by the echo of the shaft, "There's nothing to fear. No harm will come to you."

Matthew trusted Jeremy, as a friend trusts a friend. He stepped over the stone rim of the shaft and put his hand to the ladderway.

·16·

WHERE WERE THEY GOING? To the foot of Pryor's Shaft, one hundred and fifty fathoms deep? He dared not look down but kept his eyes on the sides of the shaft and the ladder. He gripped the timber staves as he had seen Jeremy do and felt with his feet, with slow deliberation, for the rungs.

One hundred and fifty fathoms, and each fathom six feet. Did the ladder descend vertically all the way? He wanted to glance down to see, but he could not. Instead he looked at the wall about him and saw nothing. He was encompassed by the dark. He could hear the dripping of the water down the shaft sides and could smell a cloying earthy smell. But he could see nothing. He could feel the staves of the ladder, smoothed by a thousand hands, but he could see nothing.

One hundred and fifty fathoms, nine hundred feet. How far had he come? He had no idea. He seemed to have been hanging in black space for hours. He called to Jeremy and his voice boomed back and back and back to him, so that he could hear the panic in his own voice repeated in the echoes.

As the last echo died softly in the shaft, falling, Matthew imagined, to the foot of it, he heard a voice beside him and his feet touched a wooden platform. It was Jeremy. They were standing together on a platform built across the shaft at the end of the first section of the ladderway. Jeremy's candle, a plume of noxious smoke rising from it, lit the area.

"You're standing on the sollar," said Jeremy. "All right?"

"All right," confirmed Matthew, and he was, while Jeremy was beside him.

"Trust me," said the boy miner. " 'Tis safe enough if you're careful. I remember four years ago when I first came down, and Dad had to lower me, he and Charles together." He paused. "I didn't like that."

He moved to the gap in the platform which led to the next section of ladder. "Keep close," he said, and stepped down.

Matthew followed, trying to move in the swift, steady way of Jeremy, but when his foot slipped on a rung and he held only by his hands to the staves until he had gotten his footing again, he moved at a slower, more cautious pace. This time the wavering flame from Jeremy's candle threw some light on the shaft walls, but it gave no comfort to Matthew, for the shadows danced and lurched till he imagined that all manner of wild creatures were descending into the abyss with him and waiting for him at the foot of it.

It seemed an age before they paused again, at the next platform. Matthew stood, still clinging to the ladder, unable to open his eyes, afraid of the shadows. He despised himself for that, but it was true; he was afraid of the shadows.

Jeremy's calm, friendly voice, soft with its Cornish accent, warm and familiar, comforted him. " 'Tis not easy the first time, but you're doing fine."

Matthew could hear sounds coming to him, almost through the rock: the striking of metal on metal, a steady thud, thud; a strange hissing, clacking noise; the noises of men and machinery. He saw, dimly illumined by the candle on Jeremy's hat, the opening of a passage from this platform, an opening lost in the dark. It was along this that the sounds were coming, reassuring sounds, for they betokened the presence of people.

"This is the thirty-fathom level," said Jeremy.

Thirty fathoms? Had they climbed down one hundred and eighty feet already?

"Along there," Jeremy gestured at the passage, "and there" — he swept his hand to indicate another — "you can get to all the shafts. Our pitch is down along from the bottom of Pryor's Shaft. We'd better move. They need me. Come along by."

He began his climb down again and Matthew followed, seeming with each step down to be gaining confidence, though he knew that danger grew with each fathom's fall. He looked up but could see nothing. He dared to look down and saw the comforting flame of the candle, but its smoke caught at his breath and made him cough so fiercely that he almost lost hold of the ladder. A feeling of panic gripped him but left him as quickly when he heard Jeremy's voice, low and safe: "Hold on now. You'll be all right."

So they descended, fathom after fathom, into the depths. At the seventy-fathom level, the noise of men and machines again boomed and sighed along the workings. To this point the shaft had been a straight drop, the ladderway vertical. Here, at the seventy-fathom level, the drive was cut slanting away, but still descending. There did not seem to be the same danger of falling, or if he let go of the ladder, thought Matthew, he would not fall plummeting to the bottom of the shaft but would slide and slither there.

Nevertheless, the descent was steep enough and tiring. His arms seemed to be tearing from their sockets with the unfamiliar exercise, and sweat was pouring down his back. When he put his hand to the rock it felt almost hot to the touch and running with water. He could hear everywhere drip upon drip into the pools that must have formed in every hollow in the rock. Water seemed to be all around him, and except for the pain in his arms he could imagine himself to be afloat.

They reached the base of the foundation and straightened up. It was wet underfoot. There was a steady flow of water along the drive they were on. Matthew now knew why the pumping engines were so important. He now knew why, once they stopped working, the mines so quickly flooded. He had a clutch of fear at the thought.

He followed Jeremy along the drive, stumbling over heaps of stone left at the sides of the narrow passage. He kept his head bent, needlessly, for even though the roof was low, it was high enough for him to walk upright, as he saw from the silhouette of Jeremy ahead. Jeremy was walking purposefully forward and Matthew could hear ahead of them the sound of metal striking upon rock, steadily, rhythmically, and the grunt of men at labor. The sounds stopped and a voice, the voice of Jeremy's father, called.

"Are you never coming, boy? We've some pretty old stuff to shift. You'd better set about it."

Matthew saw the three Visick men, resting for a moment, looking at Jeremy as he emerged from the passage. Matthew stood behind him, shy and uncertain, and was not surprised when the men paid no attention to him but spoke only to Jeremy. They had driven into the side of the passage and had cleared a kind of cavern where they were working. They seemed to have driven six or seven feet into the side. They were stripped to the waist, and runnels of sweat were coursing down their bodies. It glistened in the light of the three candles which were stuck into clay on the walls of their working.

" 'Tis awkward, boy, without 'e," said Jeremy's father. "Get some of this clear now." He indicated the rocks lying in their way on the floor of the stope, the excavation. Jeremy began to lift them, large as they were, and taking them into the drive, he loaded them into a wooden wheelbarrow.

The men returned to their work, driving into the rock. Reuben gripped the boryer, the tool for drilling, in his large hands, while his two sons, each in turn, struck it with their sledges. Matthew marveled at the steady accuracy of the strikers, but turned away to help Jeremy.

Between them they had soon filled the barrow, and Matthew watched as Jeremy slung the leather strap attached to it around his neck to support its weight, and trundled it, bumping and swaying, along the passage. At points the passage narrowed, and jutting rocks cut at Jeremy's hands. As Matthew followed him to the open area where he emptied his rock-filled barrow, he saw the blood seeping from the wounds. Jeremy seemed not to notice. Without pausing, he returned to the rock face where his father was working and began to load the barrow again.

This time Matthew slung the strap around his neck and heaved the laden barrow along the passage. The weight seemed to be tearing the middle out of him, the strap cut into his neck, his blood pounded, and when his hands caught and scraped along the side of the passage, he yelled in pain and let the barrow handles fall. The cry echoed shrilly along the workings, eerie and disturbing.

"What's wrong, boy?" Reuben Visick called, his voice filled with alarm.

"Nothing, Dad," replied Jeremy, as he lifted the barrow and continued along with it.

When he returned to the workings, Reuben looked closely at him. "Wasn't that you cried, then?"

"Why, no," said Jeremy, smiling.

"Nor did I think so," said Reuben and he looked at his older sons. " 'Tis not well."

Slowly, as if uneasy, they resumed their driving into the rock.

Matthew sat down in the shadows and watched, and nursed his bruised and bleeding hands. He was not much use to Jeremy like this, he realized. He was nesh, not man enough for the job, and he was tired. He tried to keep his eyes open but the dimness of the light, the closeness of the air, the rhythmic beat of hammer upon boryer made him drowsy, and while Jeremy continued to move rock from the stope, Matthew slept.

•17•

HIS DREAMS WERE ALL of sunlight and summer sounds, so that when he woke in the airless gloom underground he had a moment of black terror that made him catch his breath. Then he looked around and saw, next to him, Jeremy sitting back against the hard rock, taking a large flat cake from his canvas croust bag. When Jeremy saw that his eyes were open, he smiled, broke off a piece of cake, and offered it to Matthew, who shook his head. He had no appetite.

Reuben and Jeremy's brothers were also sitting, resting from their work and eating. They had doused all but one candle. There was no conversation between them. Reuben put his unfinished snack aside, took out a clay pipe which was already packed with tobacco, lit it from the candle, and sat, puffing spasmodically.

Matthew watched the puffs of smoke rise slowly and curl upward to be lost in the dark roof of the passageway. He too felt relaxed and contented, though his hands were still painful.

Charles, the taller of the brothers, was the first to move and was slowly joined by the others. They seemed to be studying the face of the rock and to be discussing their next move. Charles was clearly excited at something and pointed out a fold of rock to his father.

"I do think we've struck it rich," he said softly, with a ring of hope in his voice.

"Not before time," said his father.

They turned back from the face and began to prepare, Matthew realized, for blasting. They had driven a deep, narrow hole into the rock at the back of the stope and now John was cleaning out dust from the drill hole with a swabstick. Reuben had produced a flask of black powder. He stepped up to the hole, satisfied himself that it was clear, and then trickled powder into it. He pushed the powder home with a thin bar of metal, and when he was satisfied that the charge was laid and enough gunpowder set to blast away as much rock as was needed to reveal the streak of copper they had divined, he took the paper fuse Charles had prepared. It was a tube filled with powder and sealed with grease from the droppings of the tallow candle. He pushed a wad of clay in after the first load of powder, then slipped home the paper fuse.

He turned to his sons and beckoned them to retreat to shelter in the passage. Matthew remained, his interest caught and his awareness of danger dulled. He watched Jeremy's father take a lighted candle, set it to the fuse, and then turn and hasten to join his sons. Matthew scampered after.

They sat and waited for the blast. No blast came.

"A misfire," said Charles, and moved to rise.

"Wait longer," said Reuben firmly, and Charles settled down.

Still no blast came, and when Charles rose again to go to the rock face, Reuben and John joined him.

It was John who picked up the thin metal bar, the tamping bar, and drove it into the blast hole. There was a moment then when Matthew saw, motionless as a tableau, a set piece: the three men stooping at the face of the rock, a sudden light blazing about them as the rock burst upon them.

Black swirling smoke and dust reeled about them, surged out of the stope along the passage, and engulfed Jeremy and Matthew where they sat. Matthew's lungs retched at the fumes and his eyes smarted with pain. A deafening roar filled his ears, and then came a sudden void, an emptiness of air, followed by a rush of wind, and the flames of the candles were sucked away, and darkness was about them.

A roaring and a tumbling filled the air, and as the smoke and dust rose and fell, Matthew knew that the stope where the men had been working was now piled high with rock blasted from its sides and roof, and beneath the rock, hidden from sight, were the bodies of Reuben Visick, and of Charles and John, his sons.

Matthew turned, eyes wide with horror, to look at

Jeremy, but there was no light for him to see his companion. He put out a hand and found Jeremy's hand. Jeremy was trembling, and as Matthew touched him, he seized hold of his hand fiercely, tightly, as if holding on to life itself.

" 'Tis no use," said Jeremy to himself. "They're gone, they're gone."

As he spoke there was a further low rumble, slowly mounting until that burst into a second explosion. This time the fall of rock was from the roof of the passage, blocking their return to the ladder shaft. Though they could not see, they knew that way was closed.

Jeremy kept firm hold of Matthew's hand as he rose.

" 'Tis time to move. Us don't know when more falls will come."

Matthew followed as the boy pulled him along, scrambling over heaps of stone, into the black un-known, the only contact with life and senses the clasp of hands.

·18·

"IT'S SATURDAY. We'll let him sleep on," Susan said.

"He's a lazy young scoundrel," said Matthew's father. "Look at the time. Half past ten. He should be up and doing, Saturday or not. Not all that many years ago he'd have been earning his living, in the fields or down a mine. It would do him good to have a taste of that now."

"Oh Dad," said Janet. "You don't mean that. He's only a boy."

"You spoil him, both of you," he replied. "Well, I'm not going to stand for it. There's plenty for him to do. I'm going to turn him out of bed."

"Robert!" called his wife in protest, but was too late to stop him. He was storming up the stairs, irascible and determined to be firm.

Susan and her daughter sat waiting for the storm to erupt. They heard Matthew's bedroom door flung open, but instead of the expected cries of rage and anguish, there was silence.

Robert Clemens appeared at the door. His anger

had dropped away from him, to be replaced by a puzzled concern.

"He's not there."

Susan relaxed. "He must have gotten up early. After all, we were a bit late this morning. I expect he's gone out to the Thomases'. He'll be back soon." She poured herself another cup of tea.

"No," said Robert, still puzzled. "I was up first. The doors were all bolted on the inside."

"Front and back?" Susan was still not worried.

"Yes," Robert assured her.

Janet opened her mouth to speak, hesitated, and then asked, "Did you bolt the back door last night?"

"Yes," said her father. "I did."

"I came down in the middle of the night," said Janet, "to get myself a drink. The back door was unbolted then. I locked up. I thought you'd forgotten."

They looked at each other, none wanting to imagine the worst, but each afraid for Matthew.

"He'll not be far," said Janet. "Perhaps he went out on one of these night rambles of his and couldn't get back in."

"He's maybe sleeping in the outbuilding," Susan said and got up quickly from the table.

They went to look, but there was no sign of him. They searched in the garden under the hedgerows and in the most unlikely places, but they could not see him. Susan went into the lane and called his name, but there was no answer.

"The graveyard," said Janet. "That's where he goes." And she ran to the graveyard gate and on to the grass, among the tombs. She ran between the avenue of yews and back along the lines of monuments, calling his name. She went up to the church and found the door locked. She climbed among the vaulted graves and memorials, but there was no sign of him.

She returned home to find her father and mother at the garden gate, bewildered and anxious. She shook her head at them.

"What now?" asked Susan.

"The police?" suggested Janet tentatively.

"Too soon for that," said her father. "We'll wait till dinnertime. If I know him, he'll be back for something to eat."

They tried to reassure themselves with this, but each was uneasy. Janet felt guilty for having bolted the back door, Robert remembered with belated regret his frequent anger at the boy's misbehavior, while Susan thought anxiously of his strange excursions into the night and his obsession with the gravestone of the Visicks.

They ate their midday meal in silence, starting hopefully at every passing sound. No one had appetite for much, and though they tried to talk casually about anything but Matthew, their worries came to the surface before the meal had reached its end.

"I'm going along to see Mr. Thomas. Matthew's been there a lot lately," Susan said.

"They'd not keep him for dinner without letting us know." Robert's voice was full of his worry.

"I'm going, nonetheless," she replied, and with Janet for company walked along the lane.

"Why, no," said Mrs. Thomas. "We've not seen him at all today. Mary?" She questioned her daughter.

"No," said Mary. "I haven't seen him since yesterday afternoon."

"Was he all right then?" asked Susan.

"He'd been in a fight at school, but that was all." She remembered how quiet he had been on the way home, but that was nothing to remark about. He had often been quiet lately.

The next two hours passed slowly for the Clemens family. There seemed to be nothing to do but wait. When teatime came, Susan had no heart to put out the scones and cream and honey. If Matthew did not turn up for this, his favorite meal of the week, then something was amiss.

"I'm going to phone the police," she announced.

The police could be no help. They had had no news of any accident involving a boy. They would send out a message to look out for him, but they supposed he would turn up before nightfall. "They usually do," a comforting voice said at the other end of the line.

Susan took no comfort from it. Matthew was missing, in trouble somewhere, and she had to do something about it.

Perhaps the school might know something. She

looked for Mr. Brunskill's name in the telephone directory, but it was not there. Then she thought of that nice Mr. Williams, the history teacher. He had seemed to be sensible, whatever Robert might think. She turned to the page for Williams in the telephone directory. Her heart fell. She should have known better. There were columns of them.

She would not be defeated. She walked along the lane to the Thomas farm. Mary might know where Mr. Williams lived.

It was her father who helped, however. Interests in the history of mining had brought the two men together. They had friends in common, and after a few inquiries, the farmer ran Mr. Williams to earth.

He handed the phone to Mrs. Clemens. She rapidly explained the problem.

"I don't know what I can do to help, but I'll come round."

Shortly, with Mary Thomas and her father in attendance, the Clemenses met and conferred with George Williams.

"Why do you think it might have something to do with the school or me?" Williams asked.

Susan shook her head. "I don't know, but I had to start somewhere." Her usually bright face was pale, and worry lines aged her. Her hair was unkempt and she could not be bothered to tidy it up for Mr. Williams or anyone.

Janet intervened. She knew Mr. Williams from her own time at school, four or five years before.

"It was your lessons that set him off," she said. "It was then he started wandering to the graveyard. That's where we found him at night."

"The Martin tomb," said Williams.

"No," chirped Mary, and blushed when everyone turned to look at her. "No, another one. The Visicks."

"That's right," said her father. "He knew all about that, more than I did."

"The Visicks, of course," said Williams, remembering the written work Matthew had done.

"How does that help us?" burst out Robert Clemens. "What use is all this?"

His wife gestured angrily to him to be quiet. She wasn't sure where this was getting them, but it was better than brooding.

Their conference was interrupted by a knock on the door. Susan went to open it, and contrary emotions of hope and desperate anxiety met at the sight of the policewoman standing there.

"Is there — ?" Susan did not dare to finish her question.

"Mrs. Clemens? Your boy is still missing, then?"

The policewoman, tall, bright-eyed, and fair, joined them. George Williams explained their discussion so far.

"The Visicks," said Mr. Thomas, "seemed to interest

141

him a lot, and Wheal Maid, where the accident happened that killed the men of the family. He could tell me all about the inscription on the stone. I thought there were only three names on it, father and two sons. But he said there was a fourth, a young lad — Matthew's own age, near enough." He paused and looked at Williams. "I looked it up in the newspapers of that time. 'Twas true what he said. They reported that the body of a third son was never recovered. He's still there below, in Wheal Maid."

There was a moment's silence, then Mary found courage to speak again. Her voice was clear and showed no sign of her nervousness. What she said was the most important thing she could have said.

"That's where he is, I know. Wheal Maid."

·19·

THE OPPRESSIVE HEAT and closeness underground seemed to be made worse by the total blackness that surrounded them when Jeremy and Matthew touched their way along the drive. They heard sounds of other men from time to time at first, and the clunk of machinery. At one point Matthew was startled by the sudden thud of the pump engine. It seemed near, but as they felt their way to the noise they were met by a firm rock face. They moved slowly along it, stumbling over heaps of spoil but never once losing grip of each other's hands. They thought as they came to another passage that they would get nearer to the pumping shaft, but the noise receded and soon they could hear nothing but their own breathing and the splash and trickle of water.

Matthew's shoes were soaked from the water underfoot, and his shirt was soaked with sweat. His eyes, which could see nothing in the depths here, were tired with the effort to see. He kept opening and closing them as if that would make them work, but it was no good. There was a blackness around, of such velvet that he thought he should be able to touch it.

Only Jeremy's hand, warm and firm in its grasp, gave him courage to go on.

They came to an area where suddenly they lost contact with the rock wall. They stood together, confused, not knowing which way to turn. Matthew only knew he must try to remember which way they had come. It would be dreadful to retrace their steps and find themselves again at the rock fall.

"Jeremy," he said, and his voice echoed and re-echoed as if in a vast vaulted chamber.

"I think I know where we are," said Jeremy. "We've come to the one-hundred-fathom level, I reckon. There's a stope there twenty fathoms high, and wide too. Shout; someone might be working near at hand."

They shouted and they thought they heard an answer, but it was only the drifting echo of their voices mocking back at them.

"Let me think," said Jeremy, and pulled Matthew to the ground beside him. "I remember, I think. There's a drive goes from here, and a winze."

"A winze," said Matthew. "What's that?"

"It's a passage driven up slantwise. It joins this level with the next one up." He pulled at Matthew's hand, but Matthew, tired and drowsy, did not want to move.

"You must," said Jeremy. " 'Tis not safe to rest now."

Reluctantly Matthew let Jeremy pull him upright.

Uncertain of the space around them, they walked together first to one side, then to another of the huge cavern, their footsteps gathering in echoes about them so that they could imagine they were two of many. But they were alone. They knew now for certain. All about was stillness, broken only by the dripping of water from the rocks.

They came to one gap in the walls of the huge stope, but Matthew knew somehow, even before Jeremy turned across it, that it was the passage they had come along already. He let himself be led by the young miner. This was a more natural element to him, though for him too it must be frightening.

Matthew knew from the firm feel of Jeremy's hand that his friend had not lost hope. Though he moved slowly, groping with his free hand along the face of the cavern, he moved with purpose.

"I've got it," he said. "The winze, I'm sure."

Matthew followed him, and the sound of their footsteps changed as they moved out of the vast underground cave into the narrow passage. The ground sloped upward under them; he could tell from the extra effort he needed. He was tired, his legs and arms were aching, his eyes smarted, and breathing was difficult and shallow. The air here seemed to be thin. He heard a ghostly noise close about him and was startled until he realized it was the gasping sound of his own breath. He had to rest, whatever Jeremy thought.

Jeremy seemed to sense his weariness, for he slowed his pace and then, after a difficult scramble over the rough unseen path, he paused.

"For a moment only we'll rest. Don't go to sleep. Talk to me. Talk to me," he repeated, "so that I'll know you're awake."

"Where are we?" said Matthew when he had gotten his breath back.

"On the way up to the seventy-fathom level."

"Seventy fathoms! Still more than four hundred feet down." The despair sounded in Matthew's voice.

Jeremy clasped his hand and then Matthew felt the boy's other hand, out of the dark, touch his face. He wished he could see Jeremy's bright, cheerful smile, but though they were so close that he could feel the other's warm breath, he could only see a deeper dark in front of him, the mere imaginings of shape.

"Time to go. At the seventy-fathom level there are drives connecting all the mine. From there we can find our way to another winze and then up to the thirty-fathom level and the adit, or a ventilation shaft."

Matthew could only half understand, his brain was working so slowly. What he wanted to do was to stay there, back against the rock, and sleep. He closed his eyes and forgot all.

He felt Jeremy's hand tugging him up. "Come on. Come on." His friend's voice was urgent. "You mustn't give in." Matthew was indifferent to the plea in the voice but could not resist the strong pull on his arm. He staggered to his feet and allowed the hand to guide him on.

At one point the winze narrowed and the way steepened. They had to crawl along over the rocks and for a moment — a dreadful moment, though brief, — Matthew felt Jeremy's hand slip from his, and he was alone in the dark. He stretched out swiftly and caught a piece of stuff, the flap of Jeremy's shirt, and soon they were able to stand upright and clasp hands again.

Then they were aware that the passage had widened, the floor had leveled, and echoes of a cavern met them again.

"The seventy-fathom level," Jeremy said. "We'll find the ladder shaft." His voice sounded confident. He led the way, groping along the wall of rock.

Then he paused as if uncertain. "No. No," he muttered to himself. "It isn't." He changed direction and lost contact with the rock wall to cross the drive and touch the other side. Matthew followed, growing uneasy as he felt the uncertainty in Jeremy's movements.

"Where is it?" Jeremy said softly, as if to himself. "Where is it?" he repeated, his voice rising with the beginning of panic. He tried to free himself from Matthew, but Matthew had firm hold and would not let go.

Jeremy hurried forward, stopped and changed direction again, groped further forward, and stopped so suddenly that Matthew lurched against him.

"Where is it?" he said, and this time his young voice was hollow with despair.

·20·

"WHEAL MAID?" the policewoman said. "Where's that?"

"Over by Crofthandy," said Mr. Thomas. "But it spreads under acres of ground. There's no chimney stack as such left, no engine houses, they've all gone. There are shafts, but they're lost in the heather. He could be anywhere."

Susan who had felt a surge of hope when the name of the mine had been mentioned, refused to sink into despair.

"It's something," she said. "It's somewhere to start."

George Williams looked at Matthew's mother. He had noticed before a facial resemblance between them, but now he saw where the boy got his character.

He spoke to the policewoman. "You could get some help, I expect, while we make a start. We might find him quickly. He could have twisted an ankle or . . ."

He stopped, but Susan finished his unspoken thought for him. "Or fallen down a shaft," she said. " 'Tis possible."

149

"Ropes, blankets, thermos flasks," said Mr. Thomas, practically. "I'll put them in my Land Rover and drive us down. It's light now but it will soon be dark. We'll need lanterns. Leave all that to me."

In ten minutes he was back, ready to take them over the Downs to the heathered surface of the old mine workings. He could not resist Mary's plea to accompany them.

The sky in the west was still jade-green with light; long shadows were cast by the old engine house of Clifford and its great chimney stack. They passed the squat building that had been, so it was said, a clock tower at the center of Clifford Mines, and here they turned off the road, and along the paths, once beaten flat by packhorses, that crossed the heath and moor. They jostled and bumped against each other in the back of the Land Rover, but they hardly noticed. Nor did they speak at all, for the twists and turns and dips and rises knocked every breath from their bodies.

They drew to a stop in the midst of clumps of heather. On either side of them was a ring of stones, each marking the top of a shaft.

"Wait here," said Mr. Thomas, and he went to one shaft and George Williams to the other, and looked down. They returned to the group.

"Nothing." They reported that both shafts were filled with rubble.

For a moment they were at a loss, the waste around

them so vast and spare and dead. They were startled by the rise of a bird from near at hand. Then they began to call, long, lingering shouts of "Matthew! Matthew!" and their voices faded in the air.

They joined hands in a chain, the six of them; the three Clemenses, Mary and her father, and George Williams. They stepped warily because of the uncertain and uneven ground. They all knew that the Downs were burrowed by old miners' workings and that an incautious step might land them in a shaft. "The area is riddled with ventilation shafts and suchlike," Mr. Thomas had warned them. "Keep tight hold."

They kept tight hold and moved slowly, steadily forward, calling Matthew's name over and over again until they were hoarse. They were so intent that they did not notice the gradual descent of darkness, their eyes adjusting to the slowly fading light. But eventually they had to return to the Land Rover for the lanterns and for a hot drink from their flasks.

Susan watched the encroaching of night over the moor with growing concern. She could just make out the steeple of St. Day church on the skyline. She looked down at the shadowy gorse and heather around her. How could they search in this? Where could they search? And why had they all left the house? Suppose Matthew returned while they were out and found an empty house? Confused and conflicting thoughts rushed in and out of her anxious mind. She had to be doing something. Brooding was no good.

"Let's start again," she said. "Let's move east, toward Todpool."

They were all eager to do something and agreed. With lanterns fixed to their belts, Mr. Thomas and Mr. Williams took the ends of the lines, and holding hands again they moved cautiously on. But it was no use. The ground was too rough, their foothold too uncertain, and the uneven rocks too treacherous for their search by flashlight to be safe.

Reluctantly they turned away. As they left the Downs they met a police car with the policewoman and a police sergeant. He agreed with their judgment about a night search.

"We'll be here at first light," he said, "if the lad hasn't turned up by then."

Maybe he'll be waiting for us at home, said Susan to herself, but she was not surprised when they found the house dark and empty and cheerless.

·21·

MATTHEW CAJOLED and encouraged Jeremy but at first got no response from him. He had slumped to the floor of the drive, careless of the moisture seeping from the rocks around him. Matthew did not dare to sit down with him, for he felt certain he would sleep if he did. He could see why Jeremy had thought that was dangerous. He stood with his hand on Jeremy's shoulder. Where before it had been Jeremy who had had all the courage and he who had despaired, it was now he who had to be the guide, the leader, the strength. With the feeling of responsibility came a certainty that there was a way out from here.

Jeremy had said they were at the seventy-fathom level. That wasn't far down, he told himself, only one hundred and forty yards, not even once round a rugby pitch. That was nothing.

There must be a way out. Underground in these mines level connected with level, drive with drive; there were man shafts or ladderways, whim shafts for ore to be drawn to surface, pumping shafts for the water to be drawn from below, ventilation shafts for the supply of air to the drives: there were holes in hundreds. There was bound to be one he could find.

There were adits, too. He had heard of these and had had them pointed out to him at Perranporth and elsewhere — holes in cliffs or hillsides, giving access to the workings or providing outlets for the water.

He shook Jeremy's shoulder, put his arm down to his elbow, and lifted him up. Jeremy seemed a dead weight on his arm, but Matthew persisted and shook him again, more roughly, until he knew his friend was wakened from his dangerous drowsiness and was ready to move again.

Matthew took him by the hand. It felt cold now, with a clammy sweat, and as he clasped him tighter Matthew could feel the hard bones of his wrist.

He suddenly felt hungry and was sorry that he had not accepted Jeremy's earlier offer of a share in his hoggan, the hard dough cake he carried in his croust bag. The next time they stopped he would ask him if he had any of it left.

With one hand behind him holding onto Jeremy, he groped forward with the other against the wet rock wall. It was rough and sharp, with jagged edges of stone jutting out here and there. He struck his head against one and put up his hand to the blood that began to pour from his scalp, but though the blood trickled down his face and, salty-tasting, to his lips, it did not worry him. He healed quickly, and soon the blood dried.

His leading hand suffered and began to feel rough and tender. He ignored the pain when he felt the sharp corner of rock marking the turn of another passage. He knew as he moved into it and heard again the changed note of his footfall and felt the upward slope of the ground that it was another winze, leading surely, he thought, to the next level. Any passage moving upward was to be followed.

He moved now with more confidence but could not go any more quickly, for Jeremy's pace was slow and labored. Matthew was impatient for him to be quicker, but knew that Jeremy was held back not just by loss of strength but more by loss of hope.

What must he feel, having left his father and brothers crushed in the rock fall? How terrified he must have been, but he had not shown it, and even now, desperately tired though he was, he was moving forward slowly but surely with Matthew.

Matthew felt a new lease on life and knew he could have run up the passage to the next level, dark though it was, if he had not had responsibility for Jeremy. He had to bring Jeremy to grass, he knew. That, he saw, was why he was down here, why all this had happened.

The slope of the winze increased, and Matthew had to pause to get his breath. He could not hear Jeremy's breathing but could feel his hand within his. With his other hand he felt along and in front of him. There was a wall of rock ahead blocking the winze, a rough tumble of stones from the roof. He lost his head briefly and let go of Jeremy's hand while he scrambled frenziedly over the rocks, dislodging some noisily, to find a way through. His fingers stretched forward and he realized that by crawling down on his belly he could get over the obstacle.

He slithered back to Jeremy, who lay inert and indifferent where Matthew had loosed hold of his hand. Matthew felt about until he found both of Jeremy's hands, and moving backwards inch by inch over the tumbling rocks, he dragged Jeremy after him.

Every move was painful, the stones tearing at his clothes, his knees, his hands. Jeremy seemed unable to help, but there was little weight to his body so that Matthew was able to wriggle with him over the heap and into the winze on the other side.

He and Jeremy lay, their backs to the piled rock. Matthew put out a hand to his friend and touched the canvas food bag he carried. It felt brittle to the touch. He opened the flap and searched inside. He knew Jeremy would not mind. His fingers touched a piece of hard dry biscuit. He took it out and put it to his mouth. It was hard as the rock about them and its flavor so musty that Matthew dropped it in disgust. He felt guilty at wasting Jeremy's food, put out his hand to recover it, but could not find it. His hand felt a pool of water, cool and tempting. He knew suddenly how thirsty he was and scooped up a handful to drink. Its taste was clean and fresh. It put new heart into him.

He took hold of Jeremy's hand and dragged him upright. "We must keep moving," he said.

"Moving," came a soft reply, and Matthew was not sure if it was the echo or Jeremy who spoke.

The path seemed to level out and the rock wall to be more even to the touch. I've made it to the next level, thought Matthew. How many fathoms are we down now? He tried to remember what he knew about the workings. Who had told him? How did he know? Into his mind then came the round, friendly farmer's face of Mary's father. It was Mr. Thomas who had told him of the adit at the thirty-fathom level. The thirty-fathom level, this was it, he was certain. He wanted to let out a whoop of joy, but in the total dark that enclosed him shouts of joy seemed out of place. He choked it back, but he said calmly and confidently to Jeremy behind him, "We're almost there, I know. We're almost there."

"Almost there," was the reply, but there seemed a fading uncertainty, a query, in the answer.

We are, said Matthew to himself. I know it. He moved around the wall, feeling the surface with his fingers, until he came to a small, narrow opening. He could stretch up to feel the roof; the rock was even, smooth, almost as if worn smooth.

If it was an adit leading to the open, he would surely be able to see daylight. He took hold of Jeremy's hand and moved a few feet forward. Perhaps it was an illusion, but he thought the darkness ahead was not so intense. He thought he caught a glimmer of light — the flickering of a candle on a miner's hat, he wondered, or the flash of a lantern? Whatever it was, it confused him; it had disappeared so swiftly that he could not be sure he had not imagined it.

"Keep still," he said to Jeremy, and listened for the sound of men at work. But there was nothing except, distantly, so remote that he could not tell from which direction it came, the murmur of some engine which rose loud and then died in the dark.

His heart sank, weariness seized him, and unable to resist any longer the exhaustion that held him, he lay down and slept, his hand still clutching that of his friend.

·22·

SUSAN CLEMENS SLEPT fitfully and long before daylight was up, filling flasks with hot tea, making sandwiches, seeking to occupy her mind and body in tasks relevant to their search. She tried to avoid thinking of the likelihood of Matthew's being hurt.

Before dawn came she woke her husband and Janet, and they stood together in the morning damp waiting for Mr. Thomas. Mary was with him, in the front seat of the Land Rover. Poor child, she looks as if she hasn't slept either, thought Susan.

They had fixed a rendezvous with the police and George Williams at the little chapel at Crofthandy. As they met there and tried to unload their ropes and flasks and blankets in silence, curious eyes appeared at the cottage windows.

They walked from the village to the Downs and stood looking along the valley that separated the village from the mine workings. The morning light threw shadows differently and the landscape seemed changed from the night before.

Mary Thomas looked about her. She recognized the hillside. She had been here with Matthew when he had wanted to scramble down to explore the nooks and crannies, the holes, the rock-strewn tussocks of heather.

"I think I know," she whispered to Mr. Williams.

"Know what, Mary?" he answered.

"I think I know where he might be. We came here once before. He seemed to know just where he was going."

"Can you remember exactly?" The rest of the party had stopped to listen.

"Can we go over to the other side of the valley, please?" Mary set off without waiting for an answer and they all followed, Susan eagerly beside her.

No one spoke as Mary led the way up the road to the other side of the valley. Then, as she remembered doing with Matthew, she cut across the heather, following the tracks he had followed. She hesitated briefly at an intersection of tracks but then moved on. In a minute or two she was at the point where Matthew had stood looking down into the valley. The sides were steep and rough and pitted with hollows, some so shadowy as to be concealing shafts. Cornish heather, flowering prettily, hid the dangers lurking beneath, the holes and old man's workings that moled the earth.

They stood together and looked down, Susan's arm around Mary.

" 'Twas down there," Mary said. "He wanted to go down, but I was scared and wanted to come back. So he came with me in the end, but he was funny about it."

Susan looked at her. "Funny?"

"He didn't seem to know I was there. I should have known he'd come back."

"I'll go down," said Williams and took a step forward.

" 'Tis better for me," said one of the policemen, a young and burly constable. " 'Tis my job."

"No, it's mine," said Robert Clemens, and before the others could argue further he had climbed over the edge and slowly, watching every foothold and clinging to the heather, moved down and along the side of the hill.

He looked up once at Mary inquiringly. "Which way, Mary?" A rabbit leapt from the undergrowth and scuttled into a burrow and Robert, startled, almost lost his footing. "Which way?" he repeated.

Mary waved her arm to the right. "Over there and further down."

Robert stopped, clutching at the heather, and turned his head to look down. It was not very far to drop down the slope, but there were rocks and hidden dangers on the way.

He called, "Matthew!" and the others joined him in

the cry. "Matthew! Matthew!" The name echoed along the narrow valley. "Matthew!"

◇ ◇ ◇

Matthew wondered how long he had slept. He wondered, too, where he was and how he had gotten there. It was dark about him, but near his head he could hear a buzzing. He thought it was the buzzing of bees, but he did not think there were bees down mines. Something had wakened him, but not the buzzing.

He looked back to try to puzzle out where he was. There seemed to be a thin light about him; at least it wasn't the intense black he had feared. He stretched out his hand; someone had been with him, he remembered, but his memory was hazy. His eyes searched in the gloom; he thought he could see something, someone maybe. He saw a bundle, vague and at first shapeless, in the shadows.

He stretched out his hand further and touched the gray, huddled shape. His hand felt a brittle dry cloth that crumbled into powder as he touched it. He let his hand fall to the ground and felt the clutch of a hand at his. Jeremy, of course. It all came back with a rush.

He heard a shout from beyond somewhere and felt a breath of air different from the air he had been breathing in the shaft, the fresh, sweet air of an autumn morning. He looked ahead and could see fluttering prisms of light, shifting and changing as the daylight glistened through the heather that fell over

162

the opening of the adit. The buzzing was of insects busy at the flowers.

He turned to Jeremy. "We're there! We're there!" There was no reply.

"Jeremy, we're there! Come! Wake up! Try! Try! Try!" And he gripped his friend's hand again, thin, weak, and bony. He knew as he touched the hand, its pitiful small bones yellowed and free of flesh, that Jeremy was beyond trying, beyond waking, and had been so for more than a hundred years.

Matthew knew, nevertheless, that he had done what he had sought to do. He had found Jeremy Visick; together they had come to grass.

He heard a shout again — shouts, surely his name. "Matthew! Matthew!"

"I'm here," he called, but his mouth was parched so that the sound came thin and lost.

"Matthew! Matthew!" The shouts came again, this time, he thought, from further away.

"I'm here," he called, but again his voice, cracked and hoarse, did not carry. "I'm here," he called again faintly, and moved painfully along the narrow adit to its heather-covered opening on the hillside. "I'm here," he said again, pushing aside the prickly clump weakly. "I'm here," and knew no more.

◇ ◇ ◇

Above, at the top of the hillside, the group watched Robert Clemens working his way across the slope, clutching carefully for a hold, stopping to call his son's name from time to time and then listening, in vain, for a reply.

"He's moving the wrong way," said Mary. "He should be nearer that way." She leaned forward and pointed to the right. "He should be over there."

She looked where she had pointed. There was something there, she was certain, that had not been there before, something pale against the dark green and purple of the moor. She blinked and looked again. She did not dare to speak but clutched at Mrs. Clemens's arm and soundlessly pointed.

Susan looked and saw the fluttering of a hand.

"It's him," she called, and gathered Mary to her in a sudden access of joy. "He's there! I saw him! Mary saw him! He's there!"

She wanted to scramble down but Mr. Thomas restrained her. "We'll bring him to you, never fear."

Mr. Thomas and the young constable worked their way carefully down the hillside and joined Robert Clemens. At his wife's call he had scrambled recklessly across and lay against the ground, both hands around those of his son, weeping unashamedly.

Matthew opened his eyes and saw his father peering at him through the gaps in the heather.

"I'm sorry, Dad," he said.

He was able, they all saw with relief, to wriggle his way out of the adit and with help to get to them at the top of the slope. He sat there, head between his hands for a moment, with his mother sitting beside him, looking at him with a joy mingled with horror at the torn fingers and the slash of blood down his cheek.

"Jeremy," he said.

"Who?" she asked.

"Jeremy. Jeremy Visick." He sounded exasperated at their lack of understanding. "Down there."

"Is there someone else down there?" said the constable, and with sureness of foot, for all his size, he worked his way rapidly down to the adit.

He shone his flashlight into the narrow opening. George Williams had joined him.

"I reckon you'll find nothing there," said Williams. "Young Matthew has a thing about Jeremy Visick. He died over a hundred years back in an accident at Wheal Maid. He's buried down below. You'll find nobody there."

The constable peered into the adit again and swung his light to and fro.

"I do think you're wrong," he said, as the light shone upon the decaying clothes and the small skeleton of a boy. "I reckon we've found Jeremy Visick, what be left of him."

◆ ◆ ◆

Matthew slept for almost twenty-four hours and woke on Monday morning refreshed and, except for the bruises and scarring on his hands, bearing no trace of his adventure.

165

Susan refused to let him go to school. She looked warily at him as he lay in bed, not daring to hope he had gotten over whatever had had hold of him. She avoided talking of it when she took his breakfast to him. As he was nibbling at his fourth slice of toast and marmalade, she joined him to drink a cup of coffee at his bedside.

His face was bright and shining with health, his eyes eager, and his curly hair tumbling about his forehead in boyish untidiness. He was sitting up, whistling between bites.

He smiled guiltily at her. "I couldn't help it, Mam."

"What, love?"

"All the trouble I caused you. Over Jeremy Visick. I had to do it."

She waited for him to go on. He looked dreamily out of the window to the trees that fringed the lane. A breeze was idly stirring their branches.

"I had to do it. I knew he was buried down there and by rights he should have been with his father and his brothers. Someone had to find him." Matthew looked at his mother and wondered if she understood.

"Why you?" she asked softly.

He did not reply, but thought of Jeremy below, staring with horror at the rock fall that had destroyed his father and his brothers. Had he found his way almost to safety, in the adit, and there lost courage? Or . . .

He heard his mother repeat her question. "Why you?"

"I don't know." He too was puzzled. "But they lived here, you know, in the outbuilding. It was their cottage."

"It's too small," said his mother derisively.

"No, it wasn't," he said with the firmness of absolute knowledge. "That's where they lived. This is called Visick's field, where our house is built."

"So it is," said his mother. "I remember now."

"Perhaps that's why it had to be me." He pushed the breakfast tray aside and started to get up.

"Oh no, you don't, my lad, until I'm sure you're well again." She plumped up his pillows.

He sank back against them, not unwillingly.

"What will happen to him now?"

"Him?"

"Jeremy." He was still seeing his friend as he had known him and was almost angry when his mother replied, "Oh, I expect they'll bury them somewhere."

"Them!" he exclaimed indignantly.

"The bones, I mean."

"They must put him with his father."

"Maybe they will, after all," his mother answered, anxious again for her son.

◇ ◇ ◇

Days later, she was able to reassure him. The burial of Jeremy's bones next to the other Visick men was arranged. The policewoman arrived with the news and with two things found among the boy's rotted, ragged clothing. One was the tattered remnants of a canvas croust bag, with the name Jeremy Visick faintly visible in faded colored stitching.

The other was a piece of stone, cuprite, whose cut face matched precisely the stone that Mr. Thomas had given him, the stone from Pryor's Shaft, taken from the one-hundred-and-fifty-fathom level of Wheal Maid.

·23·

MATTHEW'S MEMORY of Wheal Maid and its workings faded. He was not sure in a few days if he had dreamed it all. When the wounds on his hands had healed, he had only the croust bag and the stone to remind him. Once or twice at night he had gotten up to look along the lane to the graveyard and the simple tombstone of the Visick men. He had no urge to go there now; he had done all that was needed. The graveyard was a peaceful place — untidy, littered as it was with the dead leaves of field maple and ash, but peaceful. It no longer matched with his mood. His mood was for action, action on the rugby field, where his reckless enthusiasm called as much blame as praise from Mr. Stevens.

"Control yourself, boy, and you'll be all right, but as 'tis you're as busy as a bee in heather, only not so productive."

"Sir," acknowledged Matthew and threw himself into the ruck again.

He thought he had forgotten Jeremy altogether,

until toward the end of term Mr. Williams talked about the employment of children in the mines. He described graphically the conditions below ground, the life of the miner, the uncertainties of it, the danger and arduous nature of the work, the long descent on the ladder walks (sometimes several hundred fathoms deep), the lung diseases the dust brought, the powder explosions that blinded men or killed them, the breaking into water that swept men to death in sudden flood, and the rock falls that buried whole pares of men.

"That's what a miner's life was like, and the young boys had to share it, maybe from the age of eight at times."

He turned to Roger Harris, whose attention seemed to have been wandering. "How would you like that kind of life, Harris?"

"I don't know, sir."

Matthew sat silent, seeing Jeremy clearly again. He smiled. He knew.